THE QUAYSIDE MURDER

Eric Ward Book 3

ROY LEWIS

D1456439

BOOKS

Revised edition 2019
Joffe Books, London
www.joffebooks.com

First published as *A Limited Vision,* 1983

Please join our mailing list for free Kindle crime thriller, detective, and mystery books and new releases.
www.joffebooks.com

NOTE TO THE READER

Please note this book is set in the early 1980s in England, a time before mobile phones and DNA testing, and when social attitudes were very different.

Every man takes the limits of his own field of vision for the limits of the world.

Schopenhauer

CHAPTER 1

He hadn't been given time to think, to collect himself. The offer that Philip Scarn had made him was numbing: and now as Eric Ward stood outside in the sunshine, waiting for the doorman to hail him a cab, he was still confused, still uncertain what precisely he had agreed to. He was also, perhaps, unwilling to concede to himself that he had been influenced by the magnitude of the retainer Scarn had offered. With bonuses, Philip Scarn had said with a sly smile. He would have been aware that for Ward it would have meant moving from a position of dependent unemployment to twenty thousand plus a year . . .

The taxi was waiting. 'Heathrow, please.'

Eric settled back in his seat, removed his dark glasses and gently rubbed his swollen eyelids. As he did so the thought of the return flight to Newcastle came to him. The trip down had been a shattering experience. The surgeon who had operated on him for glaucoma had told him he would have to protect his eyes with dark glasses for some weeks and could expect a degree of discomfort — but the atropine would prevent any serious pain. He'd told him to avoid stress, but had made no mention of flying. But the pain had started again, just as it had used to, the moment the plane lifted above Dinnington and climbed out towards the North Sea before making its slow turn above Newcastle and Durham, to head south. The shuddering had started and the pain had lanced through his skull again like a laser, sharp, clean, clinical and deadly.

When Eric had finally reached Heathrow his shirt had been damp with sweat: pain and claustrophobia had almost exhausted him. Now, as he sat in the taxi, the prospect of another such bout of agony came to him and he leaned forward, tapped on the glass between him and the driver.

'Yeah, guv?'

'I've changed my mind — make it King's Cross, please.'

'Up to you, guv'nor.'

Eric took a deep breath. A train journey would be different. In a way more tiring, longer, more contact with other people, but at least he would be able to move about, avoid the devastating feeling of enclosure he had experienced that morning in the plane, and avoid the pain that might strike again. And it might give him freedom to think.

'Bit of trouble up ahead, guv.'

The cab had just turned into Euston Road but had slowed and was pulling up. A car had come out of a side-street, it would seem, and collided with a bus. The bus had been forced to swing outwards and was now almost straddling the left-hand side of the roadway, effectively blocking it. Traffic was already piling up behind Eric's cab and horns were beginning to blare.

The cabbie glanced at the meter. 'Real bleeder, this is goin' to be. If we don't move soon, we'll really get caught. Hold on, guv'nor.'

He dragged at the wheel with both hands, revved the engine and gave a derisory grimace in the direction of a blaring motorist on his right. Then the cab wheels lurched up over the central reservation, and the taxi ran some fifty yards into a fortuitously empty right-hand lane, against the oncoming traffic, before he swung the vehicle into a right-hand turn and drew up at the kerb in the side-street. He turned, grinned at Eric.

'Will this do? I can squeeze my way through 'ere into Gray's Inn Road, and back to central London. King's Cross is goin' to be snarled for hours at this rate. You can walk from 'ere. Hunnerd yards, no more. Then dahn the steps, froo the underpass and you're in the station. Awright?'

Eric nodded, paid him the fare and left the cab.

The morning sun had brightened and as the taxi accelerated thankfully away Eric adjusted his dark glasses, and thought suddenly of Anne. If she knew he had decided to take a train back rather than fly she would have been even angrier than she was when she had dropped him earlier at the airport. She had wanted to come with him: he had wanted to assert his independence by travelling alone. Now, as he walked hesitantly along the side-street and turned into Euston Road he began to wish that she had come after all.

The noise of the blaring traffic disturbed him; the brightness of the sun disturbed him; the people hurrying along the pavement about him disturbed him. He quickened his step, in spite of the fact that through his dark glasses he could make out little more than a blur beyond fifteen feet. He knew it now, he had been reckless in taking this journey so soon. He had assumed even this morning that the pain he had experienced on the flight had been induced by claustrophobia in his weakened condition: now he was not so sure as the ache began again, the first stirrings of cat claws behind his eyes. He needed to get to the station, use some of the atropine in the privacy of the cloakroom, and he was aware of his quickened pulse as he hurried along.

A hundred yards, the taxi-driver had said. It seemed more like a mile as tension tightened the breath in Ward's chest and the old familiar nausea rose in his throat. The surgeon had discounted a return of such symptoms other than in circumstances of pressure, which he had been warned to avoid. Grimly he walked on, quickening his step but lurching slightly, until he struck someone's shoulder and spun around, uttering an apology.

The woman was unsympathetic. 'Wanna watch where yer goin', mate! Bleedin' Euston drunks!'

Behind his dark glasses his tunnel vision had become distorted: it was as though figures emerged towards him from out of a dark-stained fog. Panic was stirring in his chest and he forced himself to slow his step, breathe deeply. He stopped, put one hand against the wall.

'You awright?'

He did not want solicitude from strangers. He straightened, nodded, muttered something and began to move more slowly, but purposefully, along the street. He passed a junction, was aware of showrooms on his right, a bank, a post office, and he knew it would be a matter of only thirty or forty more yards until he reached the steps that would take him into the underpass.

He walked on, and the noise of the traffic about him grew louder and angrier. He was vaguely aware of the entry to the underpass ahead of him, a dark mass out of which people came hurrying, blurred, indistinct figures. As he neared the entry he thought of the steps and the darkness, and he hesitated, stopped, then removed his glasses.

The light lanced into his skull. The brightness of the sunshine was devastating to eyes that had been protected for the weeks since the operation, and hastily he replaced the dark glasses again before extending his hand to grip the rail. The cold iron was under his hand and his fingers slid along it as he began to walk down the steps, unwilling to let the people hurrying about him see that he was under stress. His pace was steady and he held his head up confidently, in spite of his nervousness and semi-blindness.

Then everything seemed to happen in a whirl. A young couple came giggling and struggling in play, running up the steps, emerging into his limited vision at the last moment, thrusting their way past him so that he was forced to turn, lose his grip on the handrail. He stood there for one long moment, off balance, and suddenly became aware of someone standing just behind him, waiting, tense. There was the odour of stale beer in Eric's nostrils and he half turned, but the thrusting body spun him again, the blow on his left shoulder unbalanced him. As the man cannoned into him, pushing past and hurrying down the stairs, Eric was already twisting, reaching for the handrail and the next step.

He failed to find either. He was inches short of the rail and his foot missed the edge of the next step. He felt a jarring pain in his tendon and his leg buckled. The underpass seemed to open up to meet him as he rolled and fell, and he was aware of a woman screaming as he collapsed helplessly, falling and tumbling down the steps.

His dark glasses were dashed from his eyes and crushed; he felt a knee strike him painfully in the kidneys, and he cannoned into the wall, winded, a sharp pain across the bridge of his nose. The experiences were momentary only; there was a wild series of frantic images that flashed through his brain, but the choking sensation, the breathlessness, seemed to drive them away. His head was filled with an impression, a myriad of coloured, exploding lights until, mercifully, hands were dragging at him, feet trampling about him, and a deep, dark blackness gave him release.

* * *

The request had come right out of the blue.

The phone call from Philip Scarn had been vague, noncommittal and almost mysterious in its phrasing: would Mr Ward care to come down to London to discuss possibilities of employment?

Anne had been disapproving. In her view it was still too soon for him to think of working. He was still forced to wear dark glasses, his vision was seriously impaired, he hadn't been cleared by the surgeon yet as fit to work — she pattered out the reasons for her objections but Eric found them irritating. He could not avoid the perhaps ungenerous thought that she still wanted him to be dependent upon her, and was unwilling to see him return to a semblance of normality.

But for him a swift return was becoming essential, if only to bring about a degree of self-confidence in himself. The recent years had been shattering, physically and emotionally. In the police force he had prided himself upon his fitness, and his enforced retirement through glaucoma had been a hammer blow. Then, later, to discover that surgery was necessary if he was even to continue as a solicitor had caused him a personal crisis that still cast a shadow over him.

At the same time, while he analysed her feelings, he was also forced to admit that she might be right in her assessment of his condition: paradoxically, it increased his stubbornness and made him determined to attend the interview in London. There was something to prove: he had to show he was still *alive*.

Eric had some vague inklings that Philip Scarn had a northern background or connections and he had made a telephone check on Scarn's company, Euromotor Enterprises, Ltd, but the information had been scanty. All he had learned was that Scarn had some marine engineering interests in the West Country and a string of garages in North London; beyond that, he had managed to glean nothing. So the invitation to come to London had been more than enough to whet his curiosity; intrigued at the time, he was recovered enough now from his ordeal in the plane to look forward with some eagerness to the meeting with Philip Scarn.

The taxi deposited him at the imposing entrance of the London hotel Scarn had suggested for their meeting. A uniformed doorman directed him to the reception desk; a brief phone call and he was then led to the lift. It ascended rapidly to the twelfth floor of the glass and concrete hotel building and the carpets were soft under Eric Ward's feet as he followed his guide to Suite 1203.

It was elegant, imposing, richly furnished and providing a magnificent view over Hyde Park. Its occupant was admiring that view with a glass of orange juice in his hand as Eric entered; he turned and smiled, extending his right hand in welcome. 'Mr Ward? I'm Philip Scarn. I'm delighted to meet you.'

He had an elocutionary voice, controlled in its inflections. His grip was firm, as Eric took his hand, but quickly released as though Philip Scarn feared losing something in physical contact. His sun-parched skin, that owed nothing to England, gave a brown polished background to his clean, white smile, but it was an actor's smile that left his eyes vacant. The whites of his eyes had a yellowish tinge — the result, Eric considered fancifully, of a bad digestion or a worse conscience. His hair was thin and unnaturally dark for his age-mid-fifties or so — but he would bring to his business activity the care he brought to his appearance: pale blue shirt and grey metallic tie, grey suit, grey, built-up shoes of suede: clean, unassuming, but precise. He was several inches shorter than Eric, and several inches rounder at the waist. He displayed comfort, ease and affluence — and a superficiality that Eric Ward found disturbing. Philip Scarn would be a man difficult to get to know. Sun-wrinkles creased around the man's eyes as he waved Eric towards the window.

'Magnificent view.'

'It is.'

'Far better than the one from my office in Hounslow. But one of the advantages of running a successful business is that you can conduct your interviews where you feel at ease — if they are of importance. And I feel at ease in this kind of surroundings.'

'And this interview is of importance?'

Philip Scarn flashed him a smile and sipped at his orange juice. He waved a hand, limp-wristed, deprecating. 'Forgive me, I've offered you no hospitality. You would like—?'

'An orange juice would do me fine.' Eric Ward was suddenly conscious of the fact he was still wearing dark glasses. 'It's a bit early in the morning for alcohol,' he blurted out.

Philip Scarn smiled at him vaguely and then turned to pour another glass of orange juice from the glass container near the window. 'Alcohol can be bad for one's state of mind, as well as a state of health.'

'So you know about my problems?'

'Of course. They are irrelevant. Glaucoma is a physical problem that need do little to affect the precision of a man's mind or the honesty of his intentions.'

Things were moving faster than Eric had expected. He accepted the orange juice from Scarn and sipped it: the juice was ice-cold, bringing a mild ache to his forehead. 'Is that why you've called me down here to talk?' he asked.

'Precision of intellect? Honesty?' Philip Scarn waved his glass negligently. 'There are other reasons. Tell me, Mr Ward, what do you know about me?'

Eric shrugged. 'You're chairman of Euromotor Enterprises: apart from that, I know very little about you.

Philip Scarn ran a satisfied hand over his spreading waistline and gave a considered impression of a pleased, self-congratulatory cat, purring over a captive mouse. 'Interesting. *I* know rather a lot more about *you*, Mr Ward.'

'So?'

'It's why I want you to represent me.'

'In what context?'

'Ah, now that runs a little too fast. You say you know little or nothing about me . . . but your background, your experience . . . my name means nothing to you?'

'It has . . . vague connotations.'

Philip Scarn smiled: for the first time it had an element of real, appreciative amusement in it. '"Vague connotations'. . . I like that. It suggests elements of discretion. All right, Mr Ward, let's proceed from there. Let's agree for the moment we are both . . . aware I have northern connections.'

Eric Ward sipped at his orange juice, irritably concerned at the thought that in some indefinable way he was off track, and subject to some kind of misunderstanding. Philip Scarn was wandering back towards the view he admired at the windows, one hand splay-fingered across his spreading waistline, the other gripping his glass pressed against his shoulder. 'I think I should then sketch in the scenario for you, my friend.'

'Please,' Eric said.

'I have always had a leaning towards the North. I was born in the West Country, believe it or not, and that is why I have retained, and indeed built up, my interests in that area—'

'Marine engineering.'

'—Quite so. But that is little more than a sideline, as you'll no doubt discover once you join me, and . . . get to know the scope of my operations. But that's by the way. The North, for me, holds a special place in the heart. The wild hills, the clean air . . . it is difficult to explain to someone not from the North.'

'I understand.'

'I was sure you would,' Scarn said silkily, and turned to face Eric. 'And you won't be surprised at my desire to return.'

'Return?'

'In a business sense.'

'What kind of business?'

'Ah, well, that's the point. In a sense, a *new* kind of business, as far as I'm concerned, if you know what I mean. The entertainment industry.'

Eric Ward frowned, sipped at his orange juice. 'I can't say I know very much, if anything about the entertainment business, north or south. So why—'

'What do you need to know about the *entertainment* industry? I would be employing you as a lawyer, not as a bingo-caller!'

Eric put his glass down carefully on the marble-topped round table beside the leather armchair. 'I think we'd better clarify a few things—'

Philip Scarn raised a hand; its pudginess in some way only seemed to emphasize the peremptory nature of the gesture. 'No, let me explain, Mr Ward. I have a desire to return to the North-East: it is an area of attraction for me, as you will appreciate, and it is also one which has in my belief considerable business potential. It is my intention to establish new entertainment centres in the Newcastle, Sunderland and Middlesbrough areas—'

'By entertainment centres you mean—?'

'At this point, let us not specify,' Scarn demurred. 'To some extent, that is where you would come in. The point is, as I purchase the sites — and I already have bought options on three sites in these cities — I will need careful legal advice on the various aspects of licensing with regard to these sites. Thereafter, there are matters such as the purchasing of the properties, the taking up of the options, the completion of building contracts, planning matters, change of user, a myriad activities of a legal nature that could keep a good lawyer in active employment for a number of lucrative years.' He flashed a hard smile in Eric's direction. 'I am aware of the level at which lawyers consider their activities should be remunerated.'

Eric Ward was puzzled. 'You want to take up options, open entertainment businesses in the North-East, and you want me to act as your legal representative? But there are a number of firms who already exist in Newcastle alone, who could give you what you want. Any agency in London would have acted for you — fixed you up with local contacts — why take the trouble to make contact with me, when I'm . . .'

The words died away; there was a breathing silence before Philip Scarn said, 'Unemployed?'

'Something like that,' Eric said stiffly.

Philip Scarn finished his orange juice and turned away to the windows again, to stare out over Hyde Park. 'You underestimate yourself, Mr Ward.'

'I don't think I do—'

'Believe me. I have taken advice. In the first instance, your background is, shall we say, somewhat unusual?'

'If you mean my time in the police force—'

'Precisely. I like a man with an unusual background: lawyers, particularly, can lead such sheltered lives, divorced from the realities, even though they confront them in the criminal courts every day. And secondly, I'm aware how . . . notorious you have become in recent years.'

'I'm not sure I care for the word.'

Scarn laughed. 'Shorthand for a real regard. It is perfectly clear from your recent record that you have a considerable grasp of such complicated matters as taxation.'

'My advice to Lord Morcomb before he died—'

'Was sound. My informants tell me his daughter—' Scarn paused for a moment and eyed Eric Ward speculatively; then he went on 'his daughter would seem to have profited from the advice you gave, to the benefit of herself and the estates. A knowledge of tax evasions—'

'*Avoidance.*'

Scarn waved a negligent hand. 'Avoidance . . . is very useful. Then, I heard, there is the matter of professional ethics. You know, with some precision, where the line is to be drawn.'

Eric Ward felt a coldness strike through his veins. 'I think, before we go any further, we'd better get something clear. I imagine you're referring to the action that was brought for professional negligence against Francis, Shaw and Elder, the firm I was working for before I — before I went through with surgery for glaucoma. The suggestion was made that the professional negligence was mine. That suggestion—'

'Was thrown out by the judge—'

'By the Master,' Eric corrected, 'at preliminary hearings in chambers.'

'Let's not concern ourselves with detail,' Scarn said with a trace of irritability entering his tone. 'I'm merely stressing that as far as I'm concerned, I believe you're a man who knows his way around. No—' he insisted as Eric tried to interrupt, 'let me finish. I'll be quite frank with you. There is one further consideration. You have the reputation of being a sound lawyer, skilled in areas others have thought beneath their professional dignity. And you know where the ethical line lies. Beyond that—'

'Yes?'

'Well, let's face it, you've got *contacts.*'

There was something about the remark that made Eric bridle. He glared at the shorter man, not knowing what it was that had irritated him, yet feeling in some way tarnished by the comment. 'What exactly is that supposed to mean?'

'It means I face facts,' Philip Scarn said smoothly, 'in a way maybe you don't. You're what . . . early forties? But already in danger of ending on the scrap heap. Physically ill . . . no firm to work for . . . what are you going to do? Me, I'm prepared to make you an offer others probably wouldn't . . . but it's because you have peculiar uses as far as I'm concerned. The entertainment industry can be a dirty industry, Mr Ward; its fringes house some of the muckier people you'll meet in the North-East. You know people I don't; you've been a copper, you know your way around, you've got *contacts*. And then again, the entertainment business relies on goodwill — both from the accountancy side — you know, getting the books right and also from the licensing side. And who controls licensing? The police, certainly — and you've contacts there — but the magistracy too. And don't tell me you don't have contacts there, not after working on the blue chip side of Francis, Shaw and Elder, and handling the Morcomb affair. Contacts? You're lousy with them! And they're contacts which make you, maybe, unique as far as I'm concerned.'

'I'm not at all sure—'

Philip Scarn interrupted him, waving a hand irritably, but the irritation was unreal, unreflected in the calculated silkiness of his tone. 'What would make you sure, Mr Ward? What would convince you that working for me would be to your benefit?'

'More details—'

Philip Scarn smiled with the certainty of a cynic. 'Would the detail of a retainer of . . . say . . . twenty thousand a year be enough to persuade you?' Almost contemptuously, he moved towards the decanter near the window. 'Another orange juice, Mr Ward?'

Eric Ward shook his head. The figure mentioned had shaken him; the coolness with which Scarn had suggested the sum made him vaguely suspicious. 'What precisely would you be expecting from me for such a retainer?'

Scarn smiled, raised his left hand, levelled it, dipped it in the time-honoured gesture of doubt. 'Early days, my boy, early days. Let me put it like this. You're a man of quality, a man of integrity. That is the whisper. You're the kind of man I need in my business; the kind of man who can generate confidence for me in the North-East—'

'You mean, a front man?'

Scarn allowed a pained expression to develop on his face and he waved deprecatingly. 'That suggests shady dealings, Mr Ward. Please, a little more generosity, until you hear me out! I've explained that I want your reputation, your connections and your undoubted abilities operating for me up north. Can't we just leave it at that?'

'But what would I be doing, in practical terms?' Eric insisted.

Philip Scarn shrugged. 'Well, the first operation I'd want you to carry out for me would be the completion of the option I've taken on certain premises in Collingwood Street in Newcastle. Great traditionalists, the Geordies . . . always honoured their sons, like Admiral Collingwood, Lord Eldon. Maybe one day there'll be a Scarn Square, hey?'

He laughed but Eric was unamused. 'What's the option on Collingwood Street involve?'

'Well, you know, right now it's partly warehousing, market activity, a few offices. You'll also appreciate that it's pretty central, near the Eldon Centre, decent parking arrangements—'

'But for what purpose would you be developing the property?'

Philip Scarn turned away to look out of the window. He was silent for a few moments, then raised a shoulder diffidently. 'A night-club . . . maybe.'

'*Maybe?*'

'It depends in part upon you, my friend. The licensing arrangements will have to be handled with some delicacy. There are other . . . interests in the area which may be affected, so you'd have to tread on eggs, talk to people, get the general view.' He glanced back over his shoulder to Eric and flashed a hard-edged smile. 'And then get the licence through, of course.'

'Otherwise?'

'Oh, the completion of the whole business, of course. You know what I mean. You're the lawyer. And at the same time, there's the options in Sunderland and Middlesbrough to deal with, and there's something of the same kind of problem there.'

'Other interests?'

'That's right.'

'And in each case a change of user . . . to night-club operations?'

Scarn turned back to face Eric; his eyes were cold. 'Your tone seems to contain a hint of criticism. You don't like the . . . entertainment business?'

'Establishing night-clubs can be a tricky licensing operation.'

'So? Why else do you think I'd be paying such a large retainer?'

'But—'

'There's nothing shady or illegal in all of this, Mr Ward. It's straight, legitimate business. Straight, but with degrees of difficulty which can best be dealt with by a local man who's uncommitted to other interests, holds no other professional loyalties, who knows people and is a man to be trusted. By his employer . . . and by others.'

It left Eric confused, uncertain and excited. But when he left Scarn in his office and walked out into the late morning sunshine for his return to Newcastle, he was still quite undecided.

* * *

'You're a bloody fool, Eric Ward!'

The glass of orange juice was cold in his hand and the sunshine warm on his face as he sat on the stone terrace wall

14

at Sedleigh Hall. Across the sloping meadow in front of the terrace there would be a splendid view this crisp morning, the land first dipping down to the green of the valley and then rising gradually past the rocky scar of the quarry with its rich banks of rosebay willow herb to the distant blue of the Cheviots.

It was a view imprinted on his mind ever since he had first seen it; that, and the road to Sedleigh Hall running past craggy outcrops and small black tarns, and the Hall itself: the ornamental lake encrusted with water-lilies, the bell-topped tower, the crumbling folly half hidden by silver birch. The massivity of the Doric-pillared Hall was at his back now, warm, ivy-wreathed walls gleaming in the sunlight. He could see none of it this morning, shaded by his dark glasses, but he could recall the images, strutting pheasants on the narrow tracks, the whirring and cackling of black grouse among the distant hills.

He took a deep breath. The air was clean and sharp, the light breeze bringing with it the scent of pine, and he could hear the droning of a tractor as it sliced its methodical way across the black earth of the top field beyond the river. Behind him Anne Morcomb sighed, obviously and dramatically, waiting for a reply. Eric smiled and made none.

'I *said*,' she remarked in exasperation, 'you're a bloody fool.'

'I heard you, Anne.'

'Well?'

He smiled again, turning to look at her. 'They are the precise words you used when I got back from London and I still think they cause me no reason to make a reply.' She was annoyed. She tossed her head in a disapproving manner and began to rise.

'Anne, please.'

'I meant them then as I mean them now.'

Eric reached out and took her hand. Gently he said, 'And there were things that *I* said on that occasion that I too meant.'

She fell silent.

She had been horrified when the taxi had brought him back to Sedleigh Hall that afternoon. She had been to a board meeting in Newcastle during the morning but had returned to the Hall during the afternoon and had been down at the stables when Eric had been assisted from the car. He had had an unpleasant journey back, fortunate that one of the people who had seen his fall down the steps of the underpass had been not only a doctor but also someone who could recognize the fierceness of Eric Ward's need not to be fussed over. When Eric had recovered consciousness and insisted on boarding the train the doctor, who had also been travelling north as far as York, had stayed with him, kept an eye on him while Eric, after a cup of coffee, had merely sat in his seat with his eyes closed, hand shading the light on his brow.

There had been little problem getting a taxi: the length of the journey meant a good fare, and strangely enough, though Eric was in some considerable discomfort he had not experienced the pain he might have expected.

Things changed once he got back to the Hall. It was as though all his reserves had been gathered together to prevent the collapse that occurred as soon as he had entered his room at the Hall. He sat on the bed and then blacked out; he recalled little afterwards until some time that evening, as the light faded outside, he became aware that he was in bed, with Anne sitting beside him, and he was able to discover that she had called a doctor who had diagnosed mild concussion, recommended rest — and no further long journeys for a while.

To demonstrate that he had recovered he invited her to slip into bed beside him.

Later, they had talked.

'At least this means there'll be no question of your taking this stupid job with what's his name . . . Scarn.'

'Why do you say that?'

She had risen on one elbow, and he was aware of the softness of her breast against his arm. 'Well, there's *no* way you're going to be charging up and down to London in your condition! You've had one accident through your own stubbornness in insisting on travelling alone — and the results could have been far worse than mild concussion. To fall like that . . . it's *dangerous!*'

'But I'm all right now. And besides, the job won't involve travelling to London. It's one that'll be based here in the North-East.' He had explained to her what Scarn had told him about his plans to open up entertainment centres in the area. He did not use the word night-club.

'I just don't see the point of it.'

'What do you mean?'

'You've no *need* to take a job like that.'

'I didn't say I was going to take it, yet.'

'There's no need to even contemplate it.'

'Now, Anne—'

'We could get married,' she said fiercely. She was leaning on one elbow, and he could see her dimly in the faint light, the hair softening the outline of her face, the line of her shoulder seeming to glow in the dimness and he recalled the first time he had seen her, riding down through the trees at Vixen Hill, easy, confident. When they had been introduced he had thought of her as not beautiful, but there was a liveliness about her face, a mobility that added to the regularity of her features and the honesty of her wide-spaced eyes. Some of that confidence had gone during the last two years. It shouldn't have been that way: the death of her father, the inheritance of the Morcomb estates, the need to take up the business reins where they had fallen, all these things should have brought her a maturity beyond her years. They had not done so, and Eric Ward felt a certain guilt at the thought, for he suspected it was because of him that uncertainty still ran in her veins. He had resisted her from the start: his physical condition, an earlier broken marriage while in the police force, and the twenty years' start he had on her, had all conspired to make him feel she would be making a mistake, falling in love with him. But now they were lovers .

. . and still he resisted. He had tried to explain, gently, how it couldn't really work. She was unable to understand it any more than she could appreciate his need for independence.

'And if not that,' she said, a hint of anger staining her tone, 'there's still no need to go working for this man Scarn.'

'I didn't say—'

'We're having some difficulty with the board,' she interrupted him. 'You're aware that the company solicitor, old Higgins, has always been fussy, cautious to a degree. Well, he's really holding things up at the moment. We need to raise some capital in order to take up the Dinnington options, and it seems perfectly reasonable to me that we should do so by issuing a few extra shares, which I could take up with one of the other directors—'

'The money coming from—'

'I could capitalize some of the trust funds that Daddy—'

'I can see how old Higgins wouldn't go for *that* argument too happily,' Eric interrupted. 'Not since he's a trustee as far as those funds are concerned. He does have certain duties, darling.'

'All right, but he's got no other ideas to come up with, no suggestions to make about raising capital, and the niggles he keeps having with the company accountant . . . that's where I thought you could come in.'

'How?'

'You know the trust laws backwards; you did a lot of taxation work with Francis, Shaw and Elder-you even worked on the estates before Daddy died. You could sort it all out: keep an eye on the accountant, sort out Higgins — he'd never dare cross *you*—'

'Because I'm a lawyer, or because I'm sleeping with the beneficiary of the trust and chairman — sorry, chairperson — of the company that employs him?'

'Oh hell, you're insufferable! You refuse to see—'

'Or you do, Anne,' he said firmly, twisting in the bed so that her face was inches from his. He kissed her lightly on the tip of the nose. 'Don't you see how impossible it would be? I can't work for you: inevitably, it would spill over, make a nonsense of this relationship, and indeed I'd never know really where I stood in the company. My loyalties would be divided between you as a person and the company itself; I would never know whether my advice was acceptable to the board because of its quality and relevance or because you and I are—'

'It's not that at all, really,' she interrupted, pulling away from him to lie on her back, staring at the ceiling. She was silent for several minutes. Then at last she murmured, 'I could give you a great deal, Eric.'

'I know that.'

'But not the things you really want, that's it, isn't it?'

He said nothing.

'All those stupid, masculine, self-centred things like independence, and pride . . . masquerading under the name of self-respect.'

'Anne—' he tried to draw her close, but she pulled away from him. She snuffled quietly into the pillow. 'You're a bloody fool,' she said.

Now, six days later, she had repeated the words.

* * *

He rose from the terrace wall, strolled across to the steps that led down to the gardens and finished his glass of orange juice, aware of her stiffness behind him. 'I've told you,' he said quietly. 'I've not made up my mind yet. The letter I got from Philip Scarn yesterday amounted to a firm and formal offer. I've read it, thought about it; the retainer is far more than I could have expected—'

'But you don't *need*—'

'—but I'm still not certain I'll take the job. On the other hand, after I've made some enquiries—'

'So why do you need to go into Newcastle to do that? Damn it, we're on the phone!' She rose, walked towards him, laid a hand on his arm. 'Eric, it's been good having you here

19

with me. I don't want to risk losing what we have, and I'm sorry if I'm beginning to sound like a shrew, but I *need* you, and if anything were to happen to you—'

'What's to happen to me?' he asked gently.

'That accident in London . . . it could happen again . . . and you still haven't recovered—'

'I've *recovered*. It's been almost a week; bruises gone; no after-effects. My vision is better — all right, I still get headaches, but it's *getting* better, and maybe in another week or so I can progress to tinted lenses rather than these . . . monstrosities.'

She put her arms around him suddenly, clung to him with a surprising fierceness. 'I love you,' she said. 'I can't bear the thought of your being so ill. And if you get worse, because I haven't looked after you properly—'

'Anne, please,' he soothed her. 'Get this into perspective. I have some enquiries to make, of a friend. I'm being driven into Newcastle; I'll be meeting him there; he'll be driving me back. The drives will do me good; the conversation will do me good — and I'll be taking no decision about Philip Scarn today. I tell you, there's nothing to worry about.'

He had been unable to refine the edge of impatience that had crept into his tone. She detected it, and her clasp loosened. And there it remained. He was sorry; he wanted to apologize, but an apology would possibly have made things worse. It would have been a recognition of the tension arising between them, rooted as always in his own insecurity, his own lack of belief in their relationship, or at least in the wisdom of the relationship.

He left the terrace, and in a little while the car came for him.

* * *

The tide was in at Scotswood and the mud flats of the river had disappeared so that under the bright sunshine the Tyne sparkled and gleamed in a manner that gave credence to the story that salmon were returning at last, after the industrial poisoning of the lower reaches. Since he had last visited the area, Eric noted, some building development had gone on: many of the old houses had now been gutted, some of the Victorian bow-fronted terrace houses had been renovated, given a new lease of life and, down at the boat yard, the craft had been freshly painted, pleasure boats now growing in number in spite of the general air of decrepitude in the surrounding streets. The decaying sailors' mission house had received a new lick of paint too as though it was expecting new trade, but the Tyneside Irish Club had not changed: the faded shamrock was still dull in the morning light, scrawny cats still sunned themselves in the weed-infested front garden of the Club, and the scattered empty bottles of Newcastle Brown testified to the clientele's acceptance of local tradition.

Nor had the Hydraulic Engine changed: a few of the green slates on the roof were missing and the cream-painted walls displayed cracks in the rendering, but the red-bricked windows were still hung with the same old faded curtains and the hum of noise from inside the pub was as busy as ever.

Eric Ward entered the pub, knowing as always that there would be no discernible lull in conversations, but aware, nevertheless, that the Engine would never forgive or forget his background. Coppers had never been welcome in this Scotswood pub; ex-coppers had done nothing by retirement or resignation to change the pub regulars' view of them. There was nothing overt, nothing to which Eric could ever take exception: there was merely a slight cooling of the atmosphere, the odd glance, the general feeling of resentment in the air.

He waited for a little while until his eyes grew accustomed to the light in the bar, and then he walked across to the barman. 'Jackie Parton come in yet?'

'Not yet,' the barman replied stolidly.

Eric hesitated. 'I'll have a half of lager,' he said. One would do him no harm, he calculated.

The barman stared at his dark glasses, suspicion marking his mouth as he calculated whether they might be an affectation, and then he shrugged, pulled the lager and handed it to Eric. He seemed to view the money passed over with the same suspicion as he viewed Eric's appearance.

Jackie Parton entered some five minutes later, waved, got himself a pint at the bar after shaking his head at Eric's making to rise, and then came over, beaming broadly. 'Well, bonny lad, and how are you? It's been a few months. I heard you'd gone for the knife, like. But it went arl right, then?'

'Not so bad.'

'Great,' Jackie Parton said enthusiastically. He sipped his beer with care, wrinkling his brow. 'Aye, not so bad. New landlord here; got to check the beer, you knaa.'

'He seemed to view me with a certain suspicion.'

Parton's grin seemed to split his seamed, wrinkled face. 'Aye, well, he's got decided views about poofs, like.'

'Hey?' Eric said, startled.

'Dark glasses, man, half o' lager, like, howway, you got to see the man's point of view! No matter, anyway, the eyes is gettin' along then, hey? And I heard you got yourself sorted out at last up at Sedleigh Hall. You always was a bloody fool there. You should've married the lass long ago—'

'We're not talking of marriage,' Eric said shortly.

'Aye, well, your business—'

'I wanted to have a chat, Jackie . . . get some information.'

Jackie Parton nodded; it was what he had expected. It was one of the reasons why he had suggested they meet at the Hydraulic Engine: he felt at home here. He had grown up in Scotswood, in the violent old days when it had been far different from today, but it was still his place, where he could relax, be comfortable, in spite of all that had happened to him in between. He had fought his way out of this environment as a youngster but had never truly left it behind: his career as a jockey, his success on the northern race tracks, his growing and finally intimate knowledge of every night-dub and brothel, garden party and professional luncheon on Tyneside and his acquaintanceship with the men with the money in the North, none of it had destroyed his roots. It meant that when he had finally fallen, when his career had been brutally destroyed, there had still been somewhere to come back to, people who still welcomed him, and continued to do so after his pulped face healed along with his broken ribs, and the hammering he had received that night on Dog Leap Stairs had faded into legend. Now, he took a long draught of his Newcastle Brown and smacked his lips.

'Aye, it'll do. Right, bonny lad, so what do you want to know?'

'I've been offered a job,' Eric Ward said slowly, watching the jockey's battered face with care. 'By a man called Philip Scarn.'

Jackie Parton grimaced, waited, then raised a narrow shoulder in a doubtful shrug. 'I'm supposed to know him?'

'I don't know. I wondered.'

'What line's he in?'

'Marine engineering, in the South-West. But he has local connections up here — and he spoke of a *return* to the North-East.'

There was a vaguely puzzled expression on Jackie Parton's misshapen features. He fingered his broken nose thoughtfully, then took another long pull at his beer. 'So what's the job he's offering you?'

'You might as well have a look at the letter he's sent me. It's a formal offer of a contract to act as his legal consultant, and to undertake certain transactions detailed there.'

Jackie Parton's eyes widened as he read the letter. 'He's prepared to pay you enough. Thinks you're good, bonny lad. But . . . the *entertainment* industry?'

Eric Ward explained in some detail Philip Scarn's plans for the opening of centres in Newcastle, Sunderland and Middlesbrough. He talked of the timing of the operations, the siting, and how his first task would be to start soundings about licensing arrangements. As he spoke he was aware that Jackie Parton's eyes had become hooded, as though his personality was retreating looking for cover, and his mouth had become set and hard.

'And what is it you want from me?' Parton asked at last.

'I just want you to make some enquiries round about. If Scarn has local connections, someone will know about him. I just want him sounded out. It's a bit unusual after all: for a London businessman to seek out an unemployed solicitor: there are plenty of good firms he could call on — even Francis, Shaw and Elder, for God's sake!'

'You said he explained that: he wants your taxation experience and your contacts—'

'All right, very flattering, and maybe genuine. But, at the same time . . . well, it leaves me uneasy, so I'd like to find out a bit more about him. In other words, I'd like you to root around, see if you can discover whether there's anything shady about his operation.'

'You said he didn't have no operation up here; wanted to *return.*'

'Yes, I know, but—'

'It's down south you ought to be lookin', hinny, not up here. No mileage in me workin' for you on a southern operation. All my contacts is North-East; I got no edge down there. Better you spent your money on—'

'But if he has local connections — and by that I took him to mean he'd been in business up here, there'll be some information floating around.'

Jackie Parton stared at him expressionlessly. He licked his thin lips. 'Scarn . . . the name rings no bells. If he's worked up here, it's not in the circles I moved in. I still think you'd be better starting down south—'

'I'm not really interested in southern operations,' Eric said quietly. There was something about Parton that disturbed him. The ex-jockey had always been a cheery, outgoing individual. Their friendship was now of some years' standing and it was based upon mutual respect. Jackie Parton had an unrivalled knowledge of the underworld and had also, in his heyday, had access to the large houses on Tyneside. And when Eric had left the police force he had used Jackie in a number of private investigations for Francis, Shaw and

Elder. In all that time Parton had been open, straightforward and honest in his dealings with Eric Ward. But right now something had happened; the little man was closing up on him.

'I still think that's where you should start.'

'Even if I did, you could still ask around—'

'I don't know this Scarn character—'

'What's the matter, Jackie?'

'Whaddya mean?'

'I get the feeling that while I'm talking to you, it's like you're peering out at me from behind the slats of some dusty blind. You're backing off from me, in a way you never have done before.'

Someone began to laugh at the far end of the bar, a jarring, unpleasant sound that ended with the crash of breaking glass. The landlord bellowed in remonstration across the bar, threatening a pot-bellied man with expulsion if there was any trouble, and the incident was cleared up quickly, another round ordered, the pub bar settling down.

'It's just . . . I don't think there's much I can do to help you, Mr Ward.' Jackie Parton's glance did not meet Eric's.

'And you don't want to try.'

The little man shook his head uneasily and his hands were clasped around his beer mug. 'It's not that. I . . . well, a man's got to be careful . . . protect . . . preserve his contacts. If you use them too much they can dry up, go sour. The word gets around, you get blank looks, or people just ain't there any more, you knaa? This Scarn thing—'

'But you haven't even *asked* yet! And you don't even know him.'

'Aye, well . . .' The ex-jockey lapsed into a gloomy silence. Eric Ward waited a little while, and then pushed his lager aside. 'All right, Jackie, I'm sorry I bothered you. I'll try down south as you suggest and—'

'Now, wait a minute, Mr Ward, don't get stroppy. It's just that I got a feelin' . . . aw, hell, never mind! Look, finish your drink, bonny lad, while I get meself another pint. I said

I'd run you back didn't I? Just want to have a few words with one or two fellers in the bar; you nurse that glass and I'll be back in a little while. And all right . . . I'll do this job for you.'

He rose, hurried back to the bar with his empty glass, ordered another pint and then did a swift tour of the regulars, being greeted warmly, occasionally raucously, once or twice obscenely. True to his word he returned within fifteen minutes.

'All right, lad, if there's nothing else you need to do, it's a trip out to the green lands for me and you.'

He was in good spirits as he drove Eric into Northumberland and he laughed and joked in his usual manner. Even so, there was a hint of brittleness about it, and when they finally reached Sedleigh Hall, Parton refused to come in for a drink, pleading he wasn't used to the grand life. He drove away swiftly, with a spurt of gravel, leaving Eric standing on the steps.

* * *

Eric Ward was puzzled. The request had seemed a simple one and he could not understand Jackie Parton's reluctance to undertake the enquiry he asked of him. And yet there had been more than reluctance in the little man. There was something else, something the ex-jockey had not wanted to be seen, something he had mentally hugged to himself, like a schoolboy unwilling to allow his innermost thoughts, expressed on a writing-pad, exposed. But there had been no writing-pad, just Jackie Parton's face. And eyes. And Eric Ward had caught hints in those eyes, dark movements behind curtains. He knew what was bothering Jackie Parton, knew what he was trying to conceal.

The little man was scared.

Eric Ward walked out of the bright sunlight into the echoing hall. He stood irresolutely, disturbed at what he had seen in Jackie Parton: the ex-jockey had been a courageous rider, and was known to be careless of his personal health, on the track or, later, off. And he had said he knew nothing about Philip Scarn. It was a statement Eric believed. The name was not known to Parton, but *something* had scared him.

Eric had started to walk towards the staircase when, after a few strides, he heard the telephone ring. There was a receiver on the table in the hallway so he paused, then turned sideways to pick it up. He gave his name.

There was a long pause, silence at the other end. Then the caller replaced the receiver. Puzzled, Eric waited, then shrugged, put down the phone and started for the stairs.

The phone rang again before he reached them. Irritated, he went back, picked up the phone. Once again there was a silence, and there was something about it which turned his skin cold in spite of himself, made the hairs on the back of his neck prickle.

'Look, who the hell is this?'

This time, the silence was broken. 'Is that Eric Ward?'

The voice was deep but faint, and curiously slurred as though the speaker had been drinking. Eric said, 'Yes, it's Ward.'

'The accident . . . at King's Cross. It wasn't an accident.' The silence grew around them again, drifted on for long seconds. 'Next time . . . next time, Ward, it'll be for good.'

The click as the receiver was replaced held an air of finality.

CHAPTER 2

The following Saturday evening, Anne held a dinner-party at Sedleigh Hall. She had invited members of the board of directors of her company — established three years previously, partly as the result of Eric's advice, when working for her father, that a closer view should be taken of the Morcomb lands and investments in business terms — and they included the solicitor she insisted on referring to as 'old Higgins'. He was in fact no more than sixty, and had picked up the retainer when Anne Morcomb had withdrawn her files from Francis, Shaw and Elder. It had been a small price to pay, the firm's senior partner had concluded, to get rid of the embarrassment of Eric Ward's presence.

Higgins was in one of his confidential moods after dinner and had followed Eric out on to the terrace with his brandy. He seemed eager to discuss investment details with Eric, but the eagerness was, Eric suspected, the result of some kind of pressure from Anne. Eric's response was to ask the solicitor if he had ever come across Philip Scarn in his business dealings.

'Scarn? Scarn? Rings a bell, somehow. Northern firm, you say? Now let me think. No firm of that name, and yet I have a feeling I've come across him somewhere.'

'In marine engineering, perhaps.'

Higgins shook his narrow head, sipped contemplatively at his brandy, and sighed. 'No, never had any dealings in that field. Always would have liked to, actually; you get perks, that way, like second-hand yachts from the brokers. No . . .' He cackled suddenly. 'Scarn, yes, now wait a minute. I seem to remember something. Not marine engineering, though. Quite different.'

'I'm not sure his activity up here would have been connected with the sea,' Eric said carefully. 'It could well have been an entirely different operation . . .'

'It was, if it was the Scarn I came across,' Higgins announced confidently. 'Building.'

'Building?'

'Industrial building, to be more precise.' Higgins sipped his brandy and smiled, as Colonel Haughton strolled out on the terrace to join them. One of the board, Haughton had also spent a number of years on the Northumberland bench, and had flirted from time to time with the northern political scene. 'You'll remember the firm, Colonel.'

'What firm's that, Higgins?' The colonel had the capacity to make the name sound like an insult.

'Industrial Panels, Ltd, I think they were called. Way back, late 'fifties, early 'sixties, they started springing up all over the place, companies like that. The idea was, in the housing boom, to cut costs by prefabricating units, no nonsense with bricks and so on; rather, they'd have these concrete units, slot them together, and build houses, flats, other premises in half the time and at half the cost.'

'I remember, I remember,' Colonel Haughton said, nodding. 'Always was wary of them, meself.'

'A wariness that was justified.' Higgins chuckled subserviently. 'In view of the troubles that hit most of those firms later.'

'Troubles?' Eric queried.

'You must have heard . . . even though Francis, Shaw and Elder didn't do much of that kind of work. That kind of system building as they called it, well, it left a lot to be desired. Inadequate insulation, damp-proofing, there were all sorts of problems. They're still clearing up the financial mess all over the country, where consortia of local authorities are trying to get their money back for the jerry-building that went on.'

'And Philip Scarn was involved in that kind of operation?'

'Oh no, I didn't say that,' Higgins said cautiously. 'He was managing director of a firm in the same business, called Industrial Panels, Ltd; but they were largely concerned with setting up business units, small factories, that sort of thing. Big business in the 'sixties, I remember; a good run he had, with industrial development grants pouring in and a demand for these units rising. And got out at the right time, before the recession. So he went into marine engineering, did he?'

'Building boats, hey?' the colonel supplied.

'So Scarn wasn't involved in any . . . chicanery in relation to the problems faced by that kind of industry?' Eric persisted.

'Not that I ever heard, my boy,' Higgins said, shaking his head. 'You heard something I didn't?'

'Not at all.' Eric hesitated. 'You say he got out in time . . .'

'That's right. Far as I remember, the contract I was involved with must have been about the last that his firm won. Some eight years back, maybe . . . something like that, mid—'seventies. Don't know what happened exactly; believe the firm got taken over. Mr Scarn must have taken his money and run, and that's the last I ever heard of him. Never met him, exactly . . . and then, later on, there was all the local authority nonsense about corruption and all that sort of thing—'

'Well, gentlemen,' the light voice cut across their conversation as Anne Morcomb came out on the terrace to join them. 'Talking business, at this time and under these circumstances? Trying to persuade Eric to join the board, as I've been trying for weeks?'

'Actually,' Eric said,' we were talking about Philip Scarn.'

'Nothing good, I hope.' She was wearing a pale blue evening dress and in the light that spilled on to the terrace she looked magnificent. But her tone was very cold.

* * *

Later when the others had all gone and she was sitting with Eric in the warm dimness of the library, taking a late-night drink before retiring, she had the grace to laugh and admit that she had sent out Higgins with a mission in the first instance merely to talk to Eric, discuss the investments with him, try to raise his interest in them and the company, and then, delicately, to suggest that there was enough legal work for two lawyers on the board.

'I hardly think he would have enjoyed admitting that,' Eric said.

'He wouldn't be averse to having some of the burden removed — as long as the retainer remained the same.'

She was silent for a little while then, and it was not until several minutes later that he realized she had been watching him covertly. He smiled at her, and she said quietly, 'Did it really upset you, my sending Higgins out like that?'

'Of course not; it was the kind of underhand trick I might have expected of you.'

She managed a smile in return. 'But it's been bothering you — the offer I made.'

'No.' He turned in his chair to look at her more squarely. 'Why should you think so? We talked it through; I explained why I couldn't accept-whatever happened over the Scarn proposal.'

She shrugged, vaguely unhappy. Her regular features were shadowed and he was unable to make out what lay in her eyes. 'I don't know,' she said. 'The last few days you've seemed sort of . . . restless. I had the feeling that if it wasn't the job, it might be that you wanted to . . . to go back to your cottage in Wylam.'

'I'm very comfortable here, Anne.'

She laughed indignantly. '*Comfortable*! I think you could have phrased that a bit more gallantly.'

'Comfort,' he said seriously, 'is a very important state.' She digested that thought for a little while and then drew her chair closer to his, put a hand out so that her slim fingers rested on the back of his hand. 'Then it's something else.'

'I don't know what you mean.'

'You've been preoccupied the last few days. Remember, Eric, I *watch* you. And don't try to tell me it's Scarn, or the job I've been pressing you to take . . . or even, I suspect, the glaucoma and the surgery you've gone through. You've handled that, got it by the throat, *mastered* it except for the bad times. I know about those. This is something different. You've got something bothering you; something on your mind and you've been niggling at it—'

'You're mistaken, Anne—'

'I love you, Eric. And I *know*. There are times when you've shut me out completely, your brow's been furrowed and you're concentrating on something so hard that you're unaware of what's being said, what's going on around you. I've watched you, seen it happen, and it's so different from your normal behaviour, even when you're in physical agony.'

He hadn't intended telling her. It might have been the relaxing effect of a good dinner and interesting company; it might have been the two glasses of wine he had drunk; it was possibly merely the fact that they were alone after a long day and the evening was soft outside, with that strange, blue luminosity that the Northumberland night sky commanded in the summer; it might have been merely that he needed to talk, and with her. He told her about the phone call he had received a few days earlier.

Her fingers stiffened on his hand, and then relaxed.

'A crank.'

'So I thought at first. But then . . . well, the reference to the accident threw me.'

'The fact that this . . . nut-case said it wasn't an accident? There was a note in the evening paper, you know, to the effect you'd fallen and injured yourself in London. The price of fame, or living at Sedleigh Hall!'

Eric nodded slowly. 'I suppose you're right. It could have been anyone. Let's forget it.'

She was still watching him, closely. 'Yes, it could have been anyone. But there's something else.'

He sighed, and shrugged. 'I don't know. It's just niggled at me. You see . . . whoever it was, he didn't just mention London. He quite distinctly referred to the accident at *King's Cross*.'

'So?'

'The newspapers made no mention of King's Cross at all. Just London.'

She was silent for a few moments, and then squeezed his hand impulsively. 'Oh, this is getting all melodramatic. He could just have made the assumption. I mean, if you're travelling from London to the North . . .'

'I would normally have gone by train? When I'd flown down that morning? Do you see what I'm getting at, Anne? There's something odd about it all. The inference to be drawn . . . maybe the inference the speaker wanted me to draw . . . was that in some way he had been *involved* in the . . . accident.'

'But it was an accident—'

'Well, yes, but it was all so confused, and confusing. All I remember, really, is someone pushing me, and falling. There was a smell of stale beer . . . It's not much to go on, is it? Not much to base attempted grievous bodily harm on!'

'Eric, this is silly. Even if it wasn't a crank on the phone, who would want to do you harm? I mean, shoving you down the stairs outside the station . . . and then phoning to say whatever he did say. Who on earth would want to do that?'

Eric Ward shook his head thoughtfully. Half to himself, he murmured, 'Well, I suppose there are several possibilities.'

'Darling, you can't be serious!'

He laughed, grabbed her wrists, drew her from her chair to sit in his lap. He buried his face in her neck, but she twisted away, leaning back to look at him in a certain dismay. 'No, tell me what you mean! You really think—'

'Oh, it's foolish. It's just that . . . well, last year, when all the fuss arose with Francis, Shaw and Elder, the senior partner would no doubt have taken the greatest delight in murdering me, and was only prevented, I imagine, by the fact that he expected to be the next northern Grand Master at—'

'Be *serious!*'

'Oh, all right. Look, Anne, I have to face facts. There are occasions when you work as a lawyer when you're bound to make enemies. A client always regards his own suit as the most important in legal history; he expects utmost endeavour from his lawyer, and he expects to w*in*. When he doesn't — and it's a fifty-fifty chance after all, he often is, shall we say, less than pleased?'

'But angry enough to issue *threats.*'

'Well,' Eric admitted grudgingly, 'I admit it's not usual. But there has been the odd occasion, and not least in cases involving a lot of money. Not criminal cases, oddly enough, but ones where the client hasn't succeeded under a will, for instance. Money makes them scream like hell, when they lose it.'

'But you can't think of anyone in particular?'

Eric considered for a little while, then shook his head. There was nothing he could ever have taken seriously: angry clients tended to take their next piece of business elsewhere, rather than carry out a physically-inspired vendetta, 'I can't think of anyone,' he said.

'So it *must* be a crank.'

Eric remained silent for a little while. He cast his mind back to the years before he had qualified as a solicitor. There had been the period of articles with Francis, Shaw and Elder, shortly after glaucoma had been diagnosed, and he had been forced to leave the police force. And then there had been the years in plain clothes, and before that his stint on the beat, in uniform. He had almost forgotten those times, or perhaps had deliberately thrust them aside with their memories of pain, the break-up of his marriage, the self-doubts when the first problems associated with his illness made their appearance.

'You haven't answered me,' Anne said quietly.

'I was thinking . . . about the days in the police,' he blurted out, and then almost immediately regretted the remark as her fingers tightened on his again.

'There were criminals who—'

'Now don't get panicky, Anne. All the time I spent in the force, well, there were very few threats made. You have to remember, in an odd sort of way there's only a thin line that divides coppers and villains. Most of the men who get thrown inside, they don't hold any grudges. They've taken a chance, it's an occupational risk they face, and when they're nailed, they take it . . . philosophically. They do their bird, they come out, go straight or turn to crime again, and maybe get caught again. But on the whole—'

'On the *whole* they don't bear grudges — but there are occasions?'

'Well, I suppose so,' he was forced to admit.

'And there have been men who have threatened you?'

Reluctantly, he nodded. 'Not many.'

'*How* many?'

'I guess . . . about three, as I can recall.'

'*Three*? Eric, do you hear what you're saying? You can sit there calmly, and suggest there are three people who have in the past issued threats against you, and you get pushed down some stairs and almost killed _'

'You're exaggerating.'

' — and then you get a threatening phone call, and all you do is sit there and do nothing about it!'

He managed a grin. 'So what am I supposed to do about it? Some crank calls me—'

'You could go to the police!'

'With what?'

She was silent for a little while, watching him in the dim light. There was an edge of hostility to the silence, something new to their relationship. He sipped his coffee and stared

35

out of the window; somewhere above the copse, beyond the meadows, owls hooted on their nightly prowls.

'Maybe I wouldn't sound so hysterical,' Anne said coolly, 'if I didn't think you yourself were worried.'

'I . . . I'm not worried, exactly—'

'You've been preoccupied for days,' she insisted. 'And that's made me uncomfortable. You think you've little to go to the police with. Well, there are others you can talk it over with.'

'Such as?'

'What's wrong with your little jockey friend?'

* * *

Later, in the early hours of the morning, she stood naked in front of the open bedroom window, shivering slightly as the cool night air touched her skin. Behind her, in the bed, Eric was asleep, his breathing slow and regular, no longer prey to the kind of anxiety that had seemed to be bothering him. The slow love-making in which they had indulged had lulled him, brought sleep to him, but she had been unable to sleep; she had lain there in the darkness, her mind crawling with a slow, unreasoning fear.

Shadows lay black across the stone-flagged terrace but the moon, riding high in the dark blue night air, caused the lawns to gleam palely towards the first black band of trees above the meadow. This was her home and she loved it; Eric was here with her now, and she loved him. When she was completely honest with herself she admitted that the illness that had struck him had been necessary, as far as their relationship was concerned: he would never have come to live here with her if he had not been so helpless. She ached for him in his helplessness, yet she knew that there might come a day when he overcame his physical problems, and his pride and independence would reassert themselves, together with his own insecurity about her, his own belief that he was wrong for her. She didn't want that day to come.

36

But now there was this new situation. It was something she feared she would be unable to cope with. When he had spoken of it for the first time this evening her impulse had been to run, take him away, hide from a looming danger. Fortunately, she had had more sense than to allow her panic to be apparent: after all, maybe he was right, and it was all unimportant. But she loved Eric Ward, and she needed him, and there was nothing she would not do to protect him . . . even from himself.

She stood there, silent, hardly moving, and in a little while the sky began to pale, distant hills outlining themselves against the formal dawn. Her skin was cold when she slipped back into bed, beside Eric; she avoided contact, but after a few moments he put out a hand, touched her thigh gently, compassionately, and she knew that he had not been asleep, but had been aware of her anxiety.

She snuggled close to his warm body and he put his arms around her; she tried to sleep, but three names, the names he had given her, hammered sluggishly away in the depths of her brain. They were names of people she had never known, and she hoped she would never have to know them. They were there in her brain, nevertheless, and now perhaps they would never be eradicated.

Carter, Svensson and Fenchurch.

They had the rhythm of wheels on a railway track, but there was nothing soothing about the sound.

* * *

The Sunday morning crowds had gathered on the Quayside at Newcastle early: it was a fine morning, the dawn mist having been burned off by a sun that promised to bring out the trippers to the sweep of the coast north from Shields to Bamburgh, but here on the Quayside it was business and noise and bustle.

The traders had appeared by six in the morning, to erect the weekly stalls. While the old markets in the town centre

37

had gone, overtaken by new shopping developments, the Quayside had survived because of its location, its tradition, and its intermittent activity. During the week it was quiet, traffic rarely using the road, with only the freighters to populate the quay until the pubs disgorged their patrons in the late evening. Sunday mornings were different: the colourful row of stalls with their bargaining owners, shouting their wares, extended the length of the Quayside, and crowds of shoppers and sightseers milled about among the vegetables and clothing and brass and trinkets and ice-cream and cassettes to run the gauntlet of the street traders with their insistent offers. A group of sailors on a Norwegian freighter hung over the rail, enjoying the unusual scene; across the river, on the Gateshead bank, there was no sign of activity aboard the grey corvette of the Royal Navy.

Jackie Parton stood at the corner of Sandgate, slightly elevated above the Quayside itself, and watching the crowds and the scene down towards Broad Chare and the Custom House. It was an old, familiar picture for him but one of which he never tired. Things had changed so much in Newcastle during the last ten years but some things never changed — among them his own fierce pride in being a Geordie. He watched, and he noted who was down there among the stalls, and then after a while he heard the taxi stop behind him and he turned to see Eric Ward getting out, paying the driver, glancing towards him and smiling.

'Funny place for us to meet, Jackie. Cultural visit, is that it?'

'What's the trouble, Mr Ward? Don't like to get out of bed so early Sunday mornings?'

Ward stood beside him, towering over him as he stood gripping the green-painted handrail that led down to the market. 'It's a few years more than I care to recall since I came along to the Sunday Quayside,' he said.

'That'll be in the days you was on the beat.'

'And after, for a while.'

Jackie Parton sniffed, and scratched vigorously at the inside of his left thigh. 'Same people here as ever. Don't ever seem to get any older, some of these bonny lads. Or maybe it's because they been there as nippers, growed up, and you don't notice how people change.'

'They change all right,' Ward said shortly. 'And you've got a reason for asking to meet me here.'

'Three reasons,' Jackie replied. 'The names you gave me, week ago. It was easier done than tryin' to find out any thin' about this Scarn character. Like I told you, don't know anything about him, and don't seem to be much chat around. But the other three, well, two of them was local lads, and Tynesiders, and, they have a habit, like, of not moving too far away from their roots.'

'You've traced them?' Ward asked, and Jackie Parton glanced at him in uneasy surprise. There was a suggestion of tension in the solicitor's voice that was uncharacteristic: the surgery would seem to have affected Eric Ward more than he allowed.

'Let's go on down,' Parton suggested, and led the way on his short bowed legs into the thick of the stalls and the crowds.

* * *

The stallholder was perhaps five feet six inches tall but looked shorter because of the expanse of belly which hung over his belted grey slacks. He wore a pale blue shirt, open at the neck, with a dark blue knotted silk scarf at his throat. His face was broad, his black eyes darting and lively, and his bald pate shone in the sunlight as he shouted out the bargains he held on his stall, in jeans and anoraks and packaged shirts. He was supported by two lads, identical twins, perhaps twelve years of age, darting about at the stall, jerking like puppets to the stallholder's claim regarding his unrivalled opportunities. It was difficult to believe, even though some of the packaged shirts might have fallen off the back of a lorry, that the stallholder had once been one of the wild boys from the back streets of Scotswood.

'I can't believe it,' Eric Ward muttered.

'It's Pete Carter, all right,' Jackie Parton affirmed. 'He must have put on three stone.'

'Happens to the best of us.'

'Even so . . .'

Jackie Parton stayed back as Eric Ward moved carelessly in the direction of the stall, pausing on the way to look at trinkets and shoes displayed on some of the nearby shelves. He could appreciate Ward's surprise: ten years ago Pete Carter had been well known on Tyneside as an incorrigible tearaway, one of the first to have the police hammering on his door if a garage forecourt was turned over, or a warehouse broken into at a weekend. He'd always been small fry, and regular in his habits, which had led to his spending two periods inside; but he had also had a temper which had been well-nigh uncontrollable, and there had been two occasions when he had come close to a violence that could have put him away for twenty years. It had been on the second occasion that Eric Ward had been involved.

Pete Carter would recognize Jackie Parton immediately if he approached the stall; Jackie could not be certain he'd recognize Eric Ward behind his dark glasses. He watched curiously now as Ward moved slowly towards Carter's stall. There was a concealed tension in Ward, a coiled spring of nervousness that Jackie found odd. It was as though Ward was expecting some kind of trouble, maybe the kind that had exploded years ago when he had caught Carter and Svensson on the warehouse roof, and Svensson had tried to use the iron bar. The coppers had swarmed over the roof that night and there had been a lot of screaming by Carter, threats of violence, but it had been Svensson who had pulled the longer stretch, for trying to use the bar. Carter had got off relatively lightly, and ever after had lain pretty low.

Ward had reached the stall now and was fingering a pair of jeans. One of the boys sidled up to him, said something and

Ward shook his head. For the first time Pete Carter looked at him, then away again, but next moment Jackie Parton saw the stiffness in Carter's broad shoulders, and he knew Carter had recognized Eric Ward. But he had said nothing.

Jackie thought it was time he joined Ward.

He eased his way through the crowd, acknowledging the calls he got from the stallholders who recognized him, until he reached Eric Ward's elbow. As he did so, Pete Carter turned his head, got sight of Jackie and grinned uneasily. 'Hello, Jackie. Still keepin' funny company, then?'

Eric Ward stared directly at the fat stall holder. 'Hello, Pete. Didn't realize you'd recognized me.'

'Sidlin' up to me stall like that?' Carter scoffed. 'Once a copper, always a copper, I say. Even if you change to another kind of law. 'Course I reckernized you. Flatfooted as ever.'

'Not too flatfooted to put you inside,' Eric Ward said coldly, and Jackie Parton glanced quickly at the solicitor. He could have sworn there was an edge of real hostility in Ward's voice, but of the kind designed to provoke, rather than rooted in uncontrolled reality.

Pete Carter was not easily provoked these days. 'Long time ago, Mr Ward. Water under the bridge, and all that.'

'Changed your ways, Pete?' Eric Ward mocked. 'What's brought about that conversion?'

The black, beady eyes flickered dangerously for a moment, but fat had overlaid the hot temper and he glanced at Jackie Parton, grinned, and announced, 'Family responsibilities, like.'

'Family?'

'These two nippers. Got to put 'em on the right track, haven't I? Not mine, no, but bringin' them up like they was. You'll recall Ada Savage-Arnie Savage's widow? You know, the bloke who got knocked off on the North Road. Well, I been with Ada these last six years. Goin' straight. And the kids . . . well, look for yourself.'

Jackie Parton watched Eric Ward. He knew what he would be thinking: a memory of the dark night he had faced Carter on the warehouse roof; the screamed obscenities, the violent threats; a struggle with him and the even wilder Svensson, a tearaway of seventeen; and now this fat, complaisant, sweating, middle-aged stallholder who grinned benevolently at two twelve-year-old boys working on his stall. 'Turn up for the books, ain't it, Mr Ward? But then, who knows what's aroun' the corner. Like with you for instance . . .' A hint of malice had crept into Carter's tone. 'I hear you got your own troubles. Pushed out of the force, and now some kind of doctor trouble. That's why the glasses, is that it?'

Jackie Parton was pleased to note that Eric Ward was not rising to the bait. He seemed more at ease, satisfied at what he had seen and heard. He hadn't seen fit to tell Parton why he had wanted to contact Carter, Svensson and Fenchurch, and Jackie hadn't asked. Whatever the reason, his meeting with Carter seemed to have eased his mind in some respect.

'Tell me,' Ward was saying, 'you got out some years before your mate Svensson. What happened to him, do you know?'

Pete Carter scratched a sweaty nose, and shrugged. 'Can't really say. Wasn't a local lad, you recall. Came over as a kid on a Swedish freighter and stayed, ran wild in Byker, and then—' he grinned suddenly—'fell in with the wrong kind of company. But a wild bugger, he was, real wild. If he'd caught you that night on the roof, Mr Ward, he'd have done for you.'

'He served time for it,' Ward said stonily.

'And got out about three years after me. Then . . .'

'Did he keep in touch?'

'With me? No way. Did see him once, on Tyneside, but I'd already decided — with Ada — to set the record behind me. We had nothing in common really, anyway. Last I heard he shipped out.'

'*Shipped* out?'

'Thass right. French boat, I think. Anyway, look, I got a business to run. You want that pair of bloody jeans?'

* * *

As they walked past Sandhill and the Close, and turned up into Forth Banks and Pottery Lane the two men were silent. Jackie Parton's shadow was squat and misshapen beside Eric Ward's and the ex-jockey hunched his shoulders deliberately to make it appear more so. He'd never been under any misapprehensions about his appearance, particularly since the time he'd been worked over on Dog Leap Stairs.

'So you think that's one leopard who's changed his spots?' Ward asked suddenly.

'Pete Carter? Reckon so. All the talk is, Ada's got him pinned, made him see the error of his ways. Oh, don't get me wrong, I'm damned sure he's still grifting, still got fingers in a few illegal pies, but all small stuff, supplies for his stall, that kind of thing. He's got friends who still do a bit, and maybe that's why he was a bit nervous with you around him. Beyond that—'

'And the muscle?'

Jackie Parton twisted his narrow head to stare up at Eric Ward. 'Well, I'll tell you somethin' about that. I never thought Pete Carter *was* much of a muscle man. Oh, I 'know, there was tales in the old days, but that's what they were, in my guess. Tales. Pete was brought up in Scotswood, like me; you had to be tough and show tough — and showing tough was often enough. Pete had a good line, early developed, in scare talk. He could make people back down before they laid hands on him. He had *menace*. But muscle . . . well, I got to be convinced.'

'On the warehouse roof—'

'He *talked*,' Jackie interrupted. 'He threatened you, sure, to try to make you back off. But did he actually do anything? I mean, if he'd really used muscle . . . do you think you'd have got off that roof alive, with two of them flayin' into you?'

'Svensson—'

'Now he *was* wild. And a different kettle of fish. He didn't have words. Nor much brain. A real tearaway. I reckon Pete must have held him back that night in some way, or you would really have been bashed. Well, here we are.'

They were standing at the end of a narrow, cobbled street. It had a weary old-world air about it, redolent of its Tyneside past. The gutters were dirty, a stain of oil from some battered old car engine slowly oozing its way along towards the drain, and a mangy-eared dog was reclining on the pavement. The nearest doorways were shuttered, as though they had finally refused to face the sun any longer, and paint peeled from the windows in long, faded green strips, curling in the sun. Thirty yards down the street a battered inn sign hung crazily askew from its iron stanchion. Motionless in the still, hot air, it hung uninformatively, the painted images long having been eroded by rain and sun.

Jackie Parton grinned at Eric Ward. 'It's called the Cock Up,' he announced.

'The what? How did that get past the magistrates?'

'With some difficulty. Like you,' Jackie Parton sniffed, 'they were ignorant of the origins of the term. It derives from the printing industry, you know: there used to be a firm of printers in this street and they used this pub, so it came to be named the Cock Up, in their honour. But it's a printing term: you know, where one letter in the press gets "cocked up" above the others, and out of line.'

'I'll take your word for it,' Ward said, smiling faintly. 'But why have you brought me here?'

Jackie Parton crooked his little finger and led Ward down towards the seedy-looking pub. In front of the door he stopped, and pointed. Above the door, in faded green lettering, was the name of the licensee.

'George Fenchurch,' Ward said slowly. 'So he's keeping a pub.'

'And the talk is, behavin' himself,' Jackie Parton supplied. 'I could never understand how it was he blamed you for the workin' over he got down in the cells, the night he got pulled in. But he was sure mad as hell when he pulled two years afterwards; always claimed it was a put-up job, and he swore he'd put the boot into you one day. But I think he's cooled off inside; probably forgotten all about you.'

'I was the officer in charge that day, but I had nothing to do with the mayhem that went on in that cell.' Ward paused, thinking back over the years. 'As I recall, the two constables who did it, well, one got transferred to another area, and the other was asked to resign. And you think Fenchurch hasn't borne a grudge?'

Jackie Parton shrugged and turned away, leading Ward back towards the hill. 'Who can really say what goes on in a feller's head? But it's all of six years, isn't it? And there's been no story about Fenchurch doing much other than runnin' this pub. It's little enough, but it is his own: he got a windfall on the ponies, they say, a bit of luck that set him up to buy the pub. It was like compensation for what happened to him, in a way.'

'Compensation?'

Jackie Parton screwed his little eyes against the sunlight and glanced at Eric Ward. 'That's right. You may recall, George Fenchurch was always a bit mad about motorbikes. After he came out of prison he bought himself a 500, and burned up most of the Northumberland roads. Till he came off, on the Alnwick bypass. They took his leg off a week later.' Parton paused, watching Eric Ward's face. 'That makes a difference?'

Ward was silent for a few moments and then slowly he nodded. 'It makes a difference,' he said softly.

They came back down to Skinner Burn and stood in the shadow of the Redheugh Bridge; Jackie Parton had the feeling that Eric Ward was in some way disappointed and yet relieved, a mixture of emotions that puzzled the ex-jockey. The sun was hot on their heads as they strolled along the Quayside, heading back towards the market. When they reached the Tyne Bridge, Ward stopped, and turned to face Jackie Parton. 'All right, we can forget the names I gave you. I'd like you now just to concentrate on Philip Scarn.'

Something moved slowly and unpleasantly in Jackie Parton's gut. He nodded, glanced around towards the black river. He shrugged. 'Like I said, not easy, there don't seem to be any hard information about him. But I still got some feelers out.'

Ward was watching him keenly, but said no more. After he had gone, Parton was conscious of the fact that Eric Ward had guessed he was scared.

* * *

By midday the Quayside was quiet. The stalls had mostly been taken down; a light breeze had risen, whipping discarded paper and light rubbish from the Quayside itself to join other detritus in the river. The sailors on the Norwegian freighter had come ashore to drink in one of the bars along the waterfront and Pete Carter, all gear stowed away, scratched his belly thoughtfully.

He had meant what he said to Eric Ward. The old days were gone: as his weight had increased, so had his wisdom. He was fond of the twins, and Ada Savage was, well, she was worth hanging on to. A good woman, in her way. Even so . . .

It was not a question of old habits dying hard. It was just a recognition of the realities of life on Tyneside. He had promised Ada six years ago that the tearaway days were finished, and he was sticking to that promise, but with the kind of precarious life he led, it was sensible to take precautions, take out insurance. It wasn't a matter of getting involved . . . it was a case of making sure there wouldn't be a knock at the door one night.

He told the twins he'd be back in a few minutes and made his way to the public house across the road from his stall. The public phone was not in use. He entered the booth, checked in the phone book, and then dialled a number. His hands were sweating: he wiped them on his pale blue shirt. It was a long time before anyone answered the phone.

'Yeah?'

'I . . . I want to talk to Mr O'Connor.'

'What about?'

Pete Carter hesitated. I heard . . . there's a whisper out, about a man called Eric Ward.'

There was a short silence, then: 'Wait a minute.' Carter's hands were sweating again. He wasn't sure he was doing the right thing ringing O'Connor's private number like this, talking over the phone, but on the other hand . . . He hadn't seen Johnston O'Connor in five years or more, but he could still remember the man's cold eyes, the slim, cruel fingers. It wasn't a matter of getting involved again . . .

* * *

'This is O'Connor. Who am I speaking to?'

'You may remember me, Mr O'Connor,' Carter said eagerly. 'From way back. Pete Carter.'

'Go on.'

Carter swallowed hard. 'I heard a whisper, on the stalls, that you was interested in hearing about a feller called Eric Ward.'

'So?'

'So he's been down at the market on the Quayside this morning. Wandering around with Jackie Parton. Asking questions. I . . . I thought maybe you'd like to know.'

'That's right.' O'Connor's voice had taken on a silky, satisfied tone, but it was cold as his eyes would be. 'But I don't think we should talk about this over the phone, Mr . . .'

'Carter.'

'Yes. I'll be sending someone around to see you, have a little chat. You can tell him all about it.'

'I—' Carter began nervously.

'Perhaps you know him already. An associate of mine. He's called Reilly.'

Holy Mother of God, Carter breathed to himself. Paddy Reilly. 'Yes, Mr O'Connor, I know him.'

'You'll be able to tell him all about it, won't you?'

'Yes sir' Carter said with conviction. Because he, like Johnston O'Connor, knew that if he didn't, Paddy Reilly would simply beat it out of him.

* * *

South of the city the Derwent wound its way down through Swalwell Park from the heights of the Stanhope moors, swinging to accommodate the mill race which ran parallel to it for a half mile and then narrowing into Derwent Gut before it poured its waters into the Tyne between Consett Staiths and the coal staiths of West Dunston. The industrial buildings that had been erected along the gut had seen better days; the staiths themselves had long ago outlived their usefulness with the passing of the coal trade from the Tyne and the terraced houses that clustered about Keelman's Bridge looked over a desolate wasteland of tipped rubbish, defunct colliery buildings and greening waste heaps towards the rising skyline of a rejuvenated Elswick on the north bank, in Newcastle.

It was many years since Eric Ward had been to Keelman's Bridge, even though he had crossed the Tyne often enough at Scotswood to avoid the packed traffic on the Tyne Bridge, running south. It was more dilapidated than he remembered, and somehow smaller, more enclosed as a community than he recalled. He had last driven up Whickham Bank to interview a suspect four or five years ago, and maybe he hadn't taken in his surroundings in those days as keenly as he did now. Or perhaps everything simply looked different from behind dark glasses.

He paid off the taxi-driver at the church near Ridley Gardens and began to walk along, searching for the address he had picked out from the telephone book. His conversation with Jackie Parton had been inconclusive: he might have been right about George Fenchurch, and Ward was inclined to write him off; he might also have been correct in his view of Pete Carter, though Ward reserved judgement on that one, for there had been a certain malice in Carter's eyes and voice when he spoke to Ward that suggested old scores still remained to be settled in the man's mind. There was still the feeling in Eric Ward's own mind that he was possibly over-reacting to the telephoned threat, and the whole thing might have been a prank which would not be repeated.

Nevertheless, it had bothered him, and still did: he had tried to put it down to a certain lack of balance after the operation. Even so, Anne was scared, and he owed it to her to ease her mind.

It was why he had thought of Dick Kenton.

Eric had never cared for Detective-Inspector Dick Kenton. A big, broad-shouldered man with a pudgy face and piggy eyes, he had held views about the criminal fraternity on Tyneside that were direct, forceful and lacking in any ambivalence. Kenton simply regarded them as vermin, and treated them as such. He had no room for compassion, no time for social workers, and he despised probation officers. He had held the confident view that Tyneside villains responded to only one kind of treatment, the kind of treatment the tearaways handed out themselves in the back streets of Scotswood and Byker. It was a treatment he was happy to dispense, and because he had been successful in getting convictions, the senior officers in the force had turned a blind eye to his activity until the day when he had interrogated a drunken prisoner in the night cell in Whitley Bay and had almost kicked him to death. He had been asked to resign a week later; there had been no public enquiry and no charges laid, but his career in the police force had been terminated abruptly.

It was perhaps two years or more since Eric had last seen Kenton. At that time he had been employed as a security officer at a local factory, and though critical of the whole operation, had been happy enough nevertheless, to hang on to such a steady job. Work for ex-policemen was not necessarily easy to obtain. It was somewhat surprising to Eric that Kenton was now living at Keelman's Bridge: he thought the man could have managed something rather better.

And the address he had culled from the telephone book was in one of the seedier streets straggling up the hill towards the colliery. The houses were bow-fronted, red brick and stone, with tiny, overgrown gardens in the front and sad, dilapidated doorways. Some of them had cellars which, by glancing through the iron gratings in the pavement, Eric could see were simply stacked with the accumulated rubbish of fifty years; several of them had been split into separate flats, one up, one down. The address used by Kenton was one such house, and the grubby nameplate was indecipherable; beside it, scrawled on the wall itself and nominating the upper flat, was the name he was looking for: *D. Kenton.*

The front door was open, the passageway beyond was dark and smelled of urine. The stairs were uncarpeted and the banister rail seemed shaky to the touch. There was an air of the condemned about the whole building as though it was tired of its existence and had finally accepted defeat. From down below he could hear an old man's coughing, a miner's cough, all rattle and tearing harshness. The narrow landing boasted a strip of curling, threadbare carpet; the door behind which Dick Kenton lived was painted dark brown and black. Eric raised his hand, and pressed the bell.

The depressing silence grew and extended around him until it became almost a physical presence. He pressed the bell again, and a third time. He began to turn away, assuming that there was no one inside the flat; then he heard a shuffling sound, a scrabbling at the door, and next moment the door opened, and Dick Kenton peered out at his visitor.

The man had obviously just got out of bed. He was unshaven, his thinning hair was tousled, and his little eyes were bleary, red-rimmed, but not so much with sleepiness, Eric guessed, as with the after-effects of considerable imbibing the night before. But Kenton had always prided himself on his drinking capacity, and had always been proud to demonstrate it: maybe this Saturday night had got a bit out of hand.

'Whassamarrer?' In the dim light on the stairs Kenton was unable to make out the identity of his visitor. 'Whosit?'

'Eric Ward.'

The name seemed to mean nothing to Kenton for a long moment, then, as it slowly registered his piggy eyes widened and there was a sagging of his jaw-line as he stared at Ward.

He champed for a moment as though his furred tongue was stuck to the roof of his mouth, and then, with a hint of belligerence, he asked, 'What the hell are you doing here?'

'I came for a chat,' Eric said quietly.

'Hell of a time, Sunday morning!'

'I thought you might be able to help me.'

Kenton stood there, considering, his piggy eyes fixed on Ward's features. There was an odd tension in his mouth, a nervousness that puzzled Ward, and he grew vaguely impatient as the scrutiny continued. 'Are you going to keep me standing here?' he asked.

'What do you want to talk about?'

'A man called Svensson.'

Again Kenton considered, watchfully. Then, at last, and with an undisguised reluctance, he told Eric to wait a moment. He shuffled back into the flat, closing the door; a few minutes later he reopened it. He turned, leading the way along a short passage, and Eric noted the woollen, old-fashioned dressing-gown he wore. Dick Kenton, it seemed, had fallen on bad times.

In fact, the flat was rather better furnished than Eric had been led to expect after the decrepitude of the entrance below and the uncarpeted stairs. The sitting-room was in a reasonable state of decoration, the three-piece suite, though sagging in places, was comfortable enough, and if the rest of the furniture was cheap in quality, it was serviceable and reasonably well maintained. Kenton slumped into one of the two easy chairs beside the television set, and reached shakily for a cigarette from the top of the set. 'Had a bit of a night, last night,' he mumbled. 'Couple of the lads off that corvette in the Tyne, they was splashin' the money about, hopin' to pick up some skirt. All they got was a cold; but some of us, we got more'n a few pints out of it all.' The explanation seemed to bother him somewhat, as though he felt some link had been omitted. He shrugged, lit the cigarette, drew on it and announced, 'I don't take favourably to being disturbed on Sunday mornings, Ward. So get on with it.'

'I'm surprised you let me in,' Eric said candidly, 'if you're feeling that rough.'

'You said you wanted help,' Kenton replied, but Eric sensed a certain evasiveness about the words, and he was still conscious of the general air of uneasiness about the ex-detective-inspector. Something was clearly bothering Kenton in connection with Eric's presence, and even though he had let him into the flat, he wanted him out as quickly as possible.

'So what's this about Svensson?' he asked, frowning.

'You remember him?'

'Didn't I always say I had a mind like a card index? Look, Ward, I may have left the force, and I may have been out of luck ever since, but I'm still as sharp as I ever was. You mention the name Svensson, and things click into place straight away. He was the young tearaway we caught on the roof of that warehouse, way back; he tried to open your skull with an iron bar. I got a few into that character myself, that night. We never did like fellers who wanted to use muscle on coppers, did we?'

The words had come tumbling out, almost incoherently, prodded by pride yet tinged with anxiety. Eric Ward sat down on the arm of the second easy chair. 'I wanted to find out if you'd heard anything more about him afterwards . . . or recently.'

'Svensson?' The pudgy face wore a scowl. 'Never did pay too much attention to villains once they left the patch. He did his time, did come back I heard, for a while, but then lit out from Tyneside. You . . . er . . . why you want to know?'

Eric Ward hesitated. He had not told Jackie Parton the reason for his enquiries because the man was a friend, and he had felt foolish about his suspicions; with Kenton it was different, and the audience might be a more receptive one if he told him the truth. 'The fact is, I've had a threatening phone call.'

Kenton stared at the glowing end of his cigarette. His hand was shaking slightly from the excesses of the night before, and he watched the movement with an air of unease. 'So?'

'I can think of maybe three people, during my time in the force, who said they intended to get back at me for real or imagined injury. Two of them I've already checked out: I think it's unlikely to be either of them. The third is Joe Svensson.'

'And what did this . . . threat amount to?'

'Physical harm.'

'And he's serious?'

'There's the chance he's already tried to have a crack at me.'

Kenton was staring at his cigarette again. After a short silence he struggled to his feet. 'I need a bloody drink; hair of the dog.' He shuffled his way into the kitchen, round-shouldered, then returned clutching a bottle of brown ale. He had no glass, but drank from the bottle, eyeing Ward as he did so.

'I thought,' Eric said, 'you might have heard something of him, or given me some information about where he's likely to have gone. You always did have the ear of certain of the Tyneside clientele.'

'Well, as far as that's concerned—'

He broke off abruptly as the sound came from behind Eric Ward. His glance flicked past Eric to the passageway: the scraping was the sound of a key in the Yale lock. Consternation stained Kenton's eyes as he sat there foolishly, holding the bottle in his hand. Next moment Eric realized the reason for Kenton's nervousness ever since he had arrived at the flat, as the woman entered with a bag of groceries in her hand. Kenton had been expecting her arrival, and Eric Ward knew who she was.

She had aged since he had last seen her. The flesh on her face had begun to sag, removing much of the doll-like prettiness she had once been proud of, and her hair was blacker than he recalled, too black for the lined skin of her face. She had had a good figure as a young woman, but now her breasts were heavy, her waistline thickening noticeably, and although the dress she wore was smart enough, it had a faded air about it, well-worn and slightly dated. The make-up she had used was a defiance against gathering age, an insistence upon the continued possession of youth, but it only served to emphasize that she was now approaching fifty, disliking it, and prepared to deny it at every turn. 'Hello, Dorothy,' Eric said, and rose to his feet to face her.

Dorothy Farnon stared at him in surprise for one long moment, and then her glance slipped past him to Dick Kenton. She took in his general appearance, the bottle in his hand, and she opened her mouth to speak but Kenton forestalled her. Hurriedly he said, 'He called to ask me for some help . . . about a character called Svensson. From the old days.'

The glance slipped back, disbelievingly, to Eric. She put down the bag of groceries, still staring at him. 'Well, I'm damned,' she said.

Disconcerted by the hostility in her eyes and the contempt in her voice, Eric said, 'It's been a long time, Dorothy.'

Her grey eyes were hard. 'It has that. But you seem to have come out pretty well. But then, you always did have it pretty easy, Eric. Knew the right people, hey? Like now. I hear you got it made, somewhere up in Northumberland, living the grand life.'

Kenton seemed moved to mollify her. 'Now hold on, love—'

'And you,' she interrupted scornfully. 'Did you have to take a skinful last night, just because I was out of the way? Look at you now, you're looking like a pig, not even dressed and it's all but midday, and a bottle of beer in your hand again.' She paused, breathing hard, and her glance swivelled to Eric Ward again. 'Not shocked, Eric? Not shocked to realize that me and this pig here are livin' in sin?'

The hostility was naked now, her eyes warm with it, her mouth twisting with a dislike he could not understand. He had never known her well, though her husband had been a good copper and one with whom he had worked on numerous occasions, but he had never noticed the bitterness in her then that seemed to have seared her now.

'I'm sorry, maybe I shouldn't have called. It's clearly inconvenient—'

'Oh, don't be so bloody prissy!' She paused, eyed Eric for a moment like a banker weighing up an investor, and then spoke to Kenton. 'Get on with your talk. I got some clearing up to do in the kitchen, I've no doubt.'

She moved past them into the kitchen and Kenton eyed the bottle in his hand with an uneasy air. It was clear that Dorothy Farnon was the dominant partner in the relationship, in spite of the reputation that Dick Kenton had built up in the force for being a hard man. He had obviously met his match in Mel Farnon's widow, but perhaps his situation had drained much of the confidence out of him.

Almost as though he was privy to Eric's thoughts, Dick Kenton said, 'Things haven't been so good this last year or so. You remember the job I had with Marshall's, as security officer. We had a break-in, and I got the push as a result of it. Not my fault; their bloody alarm system was useless and I told 'em so, but the management said they couldn't afford to update it. I had a few words to say when they kicked me out, believe me. Still . . .' His mouth twisted, and his piggy eyes seemed to sink even more despondently into the pudginess of his cheeks. 'Fact is, when you're out like that, with jobs so scarce on Tyneside it's bloody difficult. Who wants a fifty-year-old ex-copper, even If he is fit and strong?' He raised a tentative hand and caressed his spreading belly. 'Had a chance of a London job the other week, but when they interviewed me, they backed off, took a younger man.'

He stopped abruptly, as though the memory of his interview in London was distasteful, and he flicked a quick, suspicious glance at Eric, perhaps concerned that he might discover contempt in his listener's eyes.

'What about Svensson?' Eric asked. 'Do you think there's any chance he's back on Tyneside? Do you reckon you could do some asking around?'

Kenton grimaced, struggled to a more upright position and shook his head. 'I don't know. I haven't heard—'

'He could ask around,' Dorothy Farnon said harshly. The delights of the kitchen had obviously not been sufficiently alluring to draw her attention from Kenton and Ward. She stood in the doorway, glaring at Dick Kenton. 'He knows enough people in the grottier pubs on Tyneside to ask around, and come up with some answers too I've no doubt. But it'll cost you.'

There was a short silence. Eric looked at Dick Kenton and saw an inexplicable consternation struggling into the man s features. He was staring at Dorothy Farnon in puzzlement, but there was another shadow in his eyes, one Eric was unable to interpret. 'Now look, Dorothy,' he began, but she cut across him, speaking directly to Eric Ward.

'I think you'd better understand a few things about us,' she announced. 'You knew me in my better days, when Mel could see himself getting on in the force. Those were good days; it was a good life; Mel was a good copper. We were comfortable. But we never looked too far ahead; we didn't think too much about the future and Mel was a straight copper: he never had anything to do with the perks of the job, the handouts he could have picked up, the envelopes of goodies he could have taken by turning a blind eye. But where did it get us? You'll recall how it all ended.'

'I'm sorry, Dorothy, I know how you must—'

'Just a couple of bloody kids,' she said bitterly. 'A garage forecourt in Felling: all they got was twenty-five quid. And Mel chasing them down to Felling Shore. He was stupid, he should've called for assistance; instead he cornered them on Felling Drops, because they were just kids, and he could handle them, and it was only twenty-five quid anyway. And there they were, standing on the staiths, and Mel was talking to them, cajoling them . . . you know how he was, a great way with words.'

Dick Kenton shifted uncomfortably; he would have heard this story many times. Dorothy Farnon shook her head and her grey eyes glittered unpleasantly. 'One of them had a knife. It was all over very quick. A stomach job, they told me, and Mel didn't stand a chance. For twenty-five quid! So you see, there I was, no kids, alone, never worked for years, a widow, a pension that was worth sod all, and no prospects. Until Dick called around, and he was *someone*, but things just haven't worked out, we're pretty low, and we've nowhere to go, you know what I mean?'

'It's not all that bad,' Kenton muttered in remonstration.

'It's that bad,' she insisted. 'But you wouldn't know about that kind of situation, would you, Eric? I mean, when you left the force you'd already had the foresight to get rid of that tart of a wife of yours; and you'd also started reading law. No responsibilities, hey, and on top of that the push from the force meant you could take up a better paid job anyway, with prospects, as a solicitor. And even now, when by all accounts you got trouble with your eyes, you still come up smelling of roses. Sedleigh Hall, isn't that it? Got a lot of money, hasn't she? Oh yes, you got it made. Us, we're different, not that you'd understand. So that means if Dick helps you, does a job for you that you can't do for yourself, it's going to cost you!'

Envy burned in her eyes and marked her mouth with an unpleasant sneer. Eric stared at her, trying to recall the woman he had known fifteen years earlier, bright, pretty, lively. It was impossible, and there was a slow spreading ache beginning behind his eyes. He rose to his feet. 'I'd better go,' he said.

Dorothy Farnon stared at him for a long moment, almost puzzled, perhaps at her own vehemence. Her tongue flicked out like a pink little snake, touched her lips ruminatively, and was gone. She half turned, looked at Dick Kenton, and it was as though she was trying to communicate something to him. Kenton held her glance, and then rose, shuffling in his carpet slippers. 'I'll see you off then,' he said.

'Goodbye, Dorothy,' Eric said.

She hesitated, then nodded briefly. 'I always did talk too much. No offence taken, I hope.'

He was grateful for her regained control. He followed Dick Kenton down the passageway, and stepped out into the odours of the stairway. Kenton came out behind him, put a hand on his arm, and softly drew the door almost closed behind him. 'I'm sorry about that, Eric.'

'That's all right. She's had a rough time.'

'We both have. We been shacked up for a couple of years now, but somehow things have never got straight. But we . . . we work well enough together, usually.' Kenton's tone was mollifying, almost pleading. 'Anyway, look, what you were saying about this character Svensson . . .'

'Yes?'

'I have a feeling . . . I don't know, but there's something about him, something I heard . . . I'm not sure. But there's no reason why I can't do what you ask, you know, talk to a few people, do a bit of legwork. God knows I got plenty of time on my hands, and I got skills that could still be put to use, know what I mean?'

Eric hesitated. He could guess what was coming, but at least the ex-detective-inspector could do something he could not do for himself, as Dorothy Farnon had so brutally stated. 'I think that would be a good idea,' he said quietly.

Dick Kenton breathed in, tightening his stomach muscles, and his pudgy face split into an uneasy smile. He glanced back at the door, involuntarily, and then bobbed his head. 'I'd need to cover expenses, of course—'

'I think that shouldn't be a problem.' Eric took out his wallet. 'How much would you need to get started?'

Dick Kenton grimaced. 'Well . . . twenty-five quid, I suppose, would be enough to get out and about.'

Wordlessly Ward gave him the notes.

'I'll be in touch, Eric, soon as I get something.'

'You can ring me at Sedleigh Hall.'

The door closed softly behind him as he made his way down the dark staircase. He walked down the hill, looking for a phone-box from which he could ring for a taxi. There was a stale taste in his mouth and his throat was dry. People changed: the doll-like, confident prettiness. of Dorothy Farnon; the blustering belligerence of Dick Kenton, fawning for twenty-five pounds.

The same sum of money Mel Farnon had died for. He would not come back to Keelman's Bridge again and he hoped he would not need to have further contact with Kenton or Dorothy Farnon.

CHAPTER 3

Contact on a personal basis was one thing: to eradicate the flat in Keelman's Bridge and the odd pairing of Dick Kenton and Dorothy Farnon from his mind was another. Eric found his thoughts straying to them often during the next few days. Inadvertently, as he sat on the terrace in the sun at Sedleigh Hall, his mind switched back to the odours and the seediness of Keelman's Bridge, the jealous, envious anger that had been generated in the woman, the subservient wheedling of the man who had booted his way through the slums of Newcastle in support of what he regarded as the way of law and order. But there was something else, too.

Eric could think back and recognize the envy, the jealousy, the bitterness that the two generated in his presence, the force of the woman's personality, the comparative collapse of Dick Kenton's confidence, but there was something else in addition, a quality he was unable to define, an almost tangible feeling that had lain between the two in the flat, hanging in the air about them like a menacing storm cloud. There had been a tension at Keelman's Bridge that could have had its roots in the fact that all three of them had seen better days, but, in the view of two, Eric Ward had come off best. Yet Eric felt the tension arose from some other cause, something more basic, even primitive in its drive.

It was an uncomfortable thought, and one he did not care to dwell upon. So he sat in the sun and listened to the country sounds, and imagined the hills he could not see, heard again in his mind the capercaille above Rothbury Crags, and was content to relax and welcome Anne when she returned from her ride, or her board meeting, or her tramp around the farms.

There were no more phone calls, except one from Jackie Parton, who suggested they might meet in Newcastle some time during the coming week. Eric agreed a meeting would be possible. The best day from his point of view was Thursday. It was the day he was due to see the surgeon in Brandling Terrace.

* * *

The terrace was Victorian, curved, elegant, three-storeyed and isolated from the dual carriageway and the open moor beyond by a quiet road used only by the denizens of the terrace itself. It was no more than a quarter of a mile from the city centre and yet remained aloof in its situation; characterized by plane trees and silver birch, it boasted, discreetly, compact front gardens alive with rhododendrons and azalea, and young men with elderly sports cars, the gifts of wealthy professional fathers who had moved on to Volvos and Jaguars in mid-career, but who had remained mindful of the thrustful errors of youth. It was not the Tyneside of Jackie Parton or of Eric Ward, yet it was near the heartbeat of the City. Eric negotiated a waiting-room adorned with copies of *Newcastle Life*, a coiffured, tweed-suited wife protecting an overweight St Bernard with an amiable disposition, and found himself in the eminent surgeon's private room on the first floor of the house.

'I thought it would be better here,' the surgeon said smoothly, 'rather than the more formal atmosphere of the hospital. We can have a chat, and I can take a more leisurely look. Now, dear boy, if you'd care to remove those dark glasses . . .'

The inspection had been far from cursory. The surgeon's manner might have been old-worldly and a trifle too condescending for Eric's taste, but the skill and deftness of his touch, the precision with which he moved through the various tests to which he subjected Eric's eyes, and the confidence that oozed from him with a honeyed phrase and comment, was impressive. 'Well then, what do we make of it all?' he said at last, sitting back with a dramatic sigh.

'More to the point,' Eric said, mildly irritated at the surgeon's mannerisms, 'what do *you* make of it all?'

'Oh, we're coming along,' the surgeon said, smiling vaguely and watching Eric with an air of compassion. 'What . . . er . . . physical symptoms have you been experiencing recently?'

Eric took a deep breath, and shrugged. 'Much the same. I still get occasional headaches, of some severity; I seem to get less trouble with nausea at night, and the pain certainly has been nowhere as distressing as previously—'

'And the drugs?'

'I've kept religiously to the dosage prescribed,' Eric confirmed.

'Good. Splendid.'

'But my eyesight—'

'Ah, well, that's something else, isn't it?' The surgeon spread his smooth white hands deprecatingly. 'We can't expect miracles overnight, can we?'

'What *can* we expect?'

The surgeon was a trifle put out by the bluntness of Eric's question and his own tone sharpened. 'Mr Ward, you've just been subjected to surgery of some . . . delicacy and . . . ah . . . severity. You will recall I spelled out all the possibilities, and dangers, to you before you decided to go ahead with the operation. Now the success of any such kind of surgery depends on a number of factors, not least the patient himself. As far as I'm concerned, I can give you one assurance. The bypass was carried out with clinical accuracy, and I detect no sign of any problem arising from the work that was done in the theatre. But I did warn you that you couldn't expect some kind of fantastic improvement. Quite the opposite, in fact. The pain—'

'I'm not too much concerned by pain right now; what about my eyesight?'

'You're not so concerned by pain, now that it's largely gone,' the surgeon reprimanded. 'But the eyesight . . .' The surgeon sighed. 'We have to face facts. It's still too early for us to say that the bypass, creating the new channel for the fluid to escape, has been a complete success. Only time will give us that assurance. And, equally, only time will tell us whether you will find your sight . . . ah . . . as good as it once was.'

'At the moment, I can see very little,' Eric said harshly. 'The glasses I'm forced to wear—'

'Are necessary, dear boy. At least another month. Why take chances? I know your vision is, shall we say, peripheral at this point of time. I appreciate that you are unable to focus well, or see any distance. I know also that in any light other than the brightest — and that you cannot endure anyway — you are unable to obtain a sharp image, there is a blurring, a fuzziness — but I assure you, time will bring about considerable changes.'

'And the possibility of blindness?'

The surgeon remained silent for several seconds. When he sighed, it was a small, gusting sound in the room. 'I must admit to the possibility. I do not think it will happen. But it might. To some considerable extent, however, that depends upon you.'

'In what way?'

'You *must* relax, dear boy. You must use the drug treatment I have prescribed with an enthusiasm bordering on the religious. You must keep quiet. You must avoid the tension that arises in, for instance, personal confrontations. Your exercise should be restricted to quiet walks. In short,

Mr Ward, you must take things *easy*. If you don't . . . well, it's like walking along a motorway and crossing from one side to another. It's taking unnecessary chances. It's dicing with death . . . or in your case, that which you fear: blindness.' He paused, toying with a gold pencil on the desk in front of him. 'Have you done anything more about . . . employment?'

* * *

It was difficult to say whether the surgeon had been pleased by the answer. He had certainly approved of the fact that Eric was now living, whatever his misgivings about it, at Sedleigh Hall. While not enquiring into the relationship, he had taken for granted that Eric was being well looked after in such salubrious surroundings. He had expatiated upon the invigorating effect upon the constitution of country air and sunlight and made positive noises of approval when told of the relaxing nature of life in the Northumberland countryside. But he was somewhat reserved when Eric had told him that he had accepted the offer of employment by Philip Scarn.

'You've sent off a formal acceptance?'

'I have.'

'Hmmm. Of course, there's a lot to be said for . . . a formal commitment to employment. I mean, it gives you an aim, takes your mind of things . . . gives you a sense of *purpose*, hey? At the same time . . .'

He had questioned Eric closely about the nature of the work involved and had seemed somewhat unconvinced to learn it was something Eric could probably do standing on his head. 'That's fine, dear boy, qualified solicitor and all that. But the law, it's a bit like medicine, isn't it? I mean, one deals with *people*, and they can be so unpredictable. A medical textbook, a law textbook, it gives you facts . . . but so often a person, his mind, his body itself, doesn't behave as it should. Causes problems, you know?' He had fixed Eric with large serious eyes. 'Problems are the last things you want, Mr Ward. Believe me. The *last* thing.'

But he had not insisted that Eric withdraw from the contract with Scarn, and with admonitions ringing in his ears Eric had left Brandling Terrace to keep his appointment with Jackie Parton near Stowell Street. The surgeon's general air of wariness about the employment offered by Scarn nevertheless left Eric in an edgy frame of mind. He felt he needed to work, to end the aimless existence, the *dependent* existence to which he was committed with Anne at Sedleigh Hall, yet he was also aware of the tensions that might well arise in his new job, particularly since he himself was still far from convinced that the whole thing was as simple as it sounded. His formal acceptance had been the result of a phone call from Philip Scarn two days earlier. The businessman intended coming to Tyneside the following week; he wanted to know whether Eric would be available for a consultation; it was necessary prior to that to know whether Eric would be joining his organization; and surely he'd had time enough to think things over?

Eric replied that he had had time enough, and a formal acceptance would be in the post the next day. He had been true to his word. He was now committed to Philip Scarn and his northern enterprises.

* * *

Jackie Parton was sitting in the sun. The wooden seat was protected from the breezes which constantly swirled along the street by the grey, massive structure of the remains of the city wall, preserved with its front of greensward by a pride that retained the ancient castle, the moot hall, and a huddle of sixteenth-century cottages below the courthouse, clustered above the steep fall of the hill to the river. As Eric Ward approached, Jackie Parton turned to him, his face as lean and weathered as it had been during his riding days, and his grin as cheeky and infectious as the lopsided scar on his lip would allow. 'So what's the news?'

'From the surgeon?' Eric hesitated, then sat down beside the ex-jockey, stretched out his legs and looked around him, aware more than ever of the constraints imposed upon him by his illness. 'He reckons there's a good chance.'

'And the glasses?'

'Another month. Maybe longer.'

'But the operation was a success?' Parton insisted.

'You could say that. But . . . well, he warned me that I can never expect a return to the way things had been, before this damned glaucoma struck. He had a phrase for it,' Eric said grimly. 'He said I could expect to see all right but my vision would be somewhat curtailed, limited. A limited vision.'

'Better than blindness,' Jackie Parton said bluntly. Eric Ward made no reply. He sat beside the little man, thinking. The surgeon had said he should avoid stress: where did one fit into a category the kind of anxiety that had been induced by that damned telephone call? Easy to dismiss it as the work of a crank, but Eric could still remember the way the hairs had risen on the nape of his neck. He shuddered slightly, then turned to address Jackie Parton.

'And what about you? You said we ought to meet.'

'That's right.' Jackie Parton looked away down Stowell Street, to where the traffic pulsed in along the Westgate Road. 'Things have changed in this area of recent years — you noticed?'

'Can't say I have.'

'Believe me. People have moved out: you know, lots of the properties north of here used to be lived in. Not now. City centres kind of die with development, don't they? No people; just shops; and shops are dead at night.'

'So?'

'So the area's changed.' Abruptly, Jackie Parton seemed to switch the subject. 'I been askin' around about your friend, Mr Scarn—'

'My *employer*, Mr Scarn.'

'So you took the job? Well, seems okay, far as I can make out. Don't think there's any great problems in the background. All the probes I put out, he came out clean. If silence is clean, that is.'

'How do you mean?'

Jackie Parton grimaced, twisting his scarred lip. 'Well, he was in business up here all right; industrial building. But got out. Something rapid about the move, but no whispers. Good business practice, they reckon. He saw the problems coming, so got the hell out of it.'

'No skulduggery in the background?'

'Not that I can find. At the same time . . .' Parton paused uneasily, and scratched one foot against the other. 'I got a feelin' . . .'

'Tell me.'

Parton shook his head and was silent for a little while. 'If you'd spent the last few years like I have, moochin' around, talking, chattin', picking up odd bits of information here and there, you'd begin to get the kind of feel I have about things. It's not something you can easily put into words, but it's like a hair in the back of your throat, you know? You can't quite make out what it is or where exactly it is; but it's there, and while it isn't serious, it's uncomfortable. I got an uncomfortable feeling about this Philip Scarn character.'

'Why?'

'If I knew, I'd tell you!' Parton burst out irritably. Eric Ward watched the little man silently. The outburst had been uncharacteristic, and it only confirmed in Eric's mind the fact that Parton had been uneasy, and more than uneasy, about this assignment right from the beginning. He was still edgy, still nervous about something, and it was affecting his temper.

After a little while, Eric asked, 'What's this all about Jackie?'

'What do you mean?'

Quietly Eric said, 'You're scared about something.'

It was a full minute before the ex-jockey replied, and his tone was, constrained. 'Scared, maybe. Worried, anxious, I don't know the right word. All I do know . . . look, I'll come clean. You know a lot about me.' He fingered his broken nose, touched his scarred lip. 'And you know how I came by this.'

'Some kind of fracas, near Dog Leap Stairs.'

'*Fracas*! Bloody hell, that's one way to describe it! I nearly got killed . . . The fact is, as anyone will tell you, I had a pretty good thing going in the old days. I rode the northern tracks and I had a damn good record: Wetherby, York, Newcastle, Haydock Park — I got the confidence of the owners after the first few years and I was getting good rides, earnin' a hell of a lot of money, and gettin' wined and dined all over the place. Scotswood and Byker were backing me, and the champagne set were putting their shirts on me. I was riding well, and high.'

'I heard.'

'You also heard how it all fell apart. It began with a steward's enquiry at York.' Parton sniffed reflectively 'I didn't pull that race: I was aboard Gay Steward, and that's a hell of a name for a horse these days, and pulled up lame. I got hauled before the enquiry, and they didn't like it, but there was nothing to prove, and if the betting syndicate did make a bomb, there was damn all they could do about it. But not long after, there was the enquiry at Newcastle . . .' The little man fell silent for a while as he went over in his mind the events of the past. 'Once again, there was nothing to prove, but the rumour was out that I was somehow tied in with the syndicate. It was never true, believe me, but rumour . . . And then . . . you know how off-course betting works?'

'Roughly.'

'It involves careful rushes at the betting shops, timed so the price doesn't drop too drastically on course. It also needs two other things to be successful: poor communications to the course itself, and a racing certainty.'

'Is there such a thing as a racing certainty?'

Jackie Parton grinned. 'More often than you'd credit.

Still, I was at Wetherby that year, and I was under pressure to produce . . . well, let's just say there was a racing certainty, and my horse wasn't it.'

'And—'

'I didn't have the heart to pull him. He was a beautiful horse; he got his nose up and he *went*. I didn't have to do a thing. He sailed through, broke the others at three furlongs. All over bar the shouting. And the syndicate lost a packet. After that . . . well, they decided they couldn't afford me, and a lesson was needed for other uncooperative jocks. Dog Leap Stairs was the answer. I got a going-over that put me in hospital and it finished my riding days. Not physically, maybe, but there was no owner who'd take a chance after that. They pulped, mashed my face; scarred my mouth; broke more than a few bones. And killed me off as a rider.'

Carefully Eric said, 'What's all this got to do with Philip Scarn?'

'Nothing, as far as I know. But the men who worked me over, they were employed by Johnston O'Connor. Now you won't know too much about him, he keeps his head down, but take my word for it, he's an organizer on Tyneside, and big with the syndicate at the tracks. It was he who stretched me out on Dog Leap Stairs.'

'But Scarn—'

'You told me Scarn was employing you to do some work, up here on Tyneside, to set up contracts in the entertainment industry. Now it may be Scarn is naive; it may be he knows the score; I wouldn't know. He's clean, it seems. But doesn't he know that O'Connor has a controlling interest in the entertainment business up here?'

Slowly Eric Ward said, 'You think there could be trouble.'

'I know O'Connor. That Irish bastard loves trouble. And when you asked me to do some sniffing for you, about Scarn, that was one thing: but to be told what he's moving into, that's another. I've no desire to be found in the Tyne one dark night, short of a hell of a lot of breath.'

'That's why you were scared.'

'*Nervous*,' Parton corrected him. 'But I asked around and there's nothing. Down this area, like I said, it's changed a lot. No people. But the clubs operate here. Some legitimate; others not. Further west, there's the whorehouses. Where's Scarn's properties going to be bought up? What's he mean by *entertainment*? I tell you this, if he uses the same meaning as O'Connor, and if he's thinking of coming into the west end of the city, there could be some nasty surprises in store for him. And there's another thing.'

'What's that?' Eric asked.

The ex-jockey fluttered his lean fingers uncertainly. 'I don't know. Nobody's *saying* anything. I told you I heard nothing about Scarn. But I should have picked up *something*. I didn't. He's clean; but no one is saying anything at all, and that's not natural. I tell you, there's a kind of tension at the moment; I got some police contacts, you know? They won't even talk to me. Some kind of fist is on the table and it makes me uneasy. Everyone is keeping his mouth shut. And that just ain't . . . *natural*.'

Jackie Parton fell silent, staring down Stowell Street moodily, as though reflecting upon days when life had been simpler and there had been the excitement of horseflesh and the sound of the crowds. His uneasiness had communicated itself to Eric Ward, however, and it was difficult to discard in spite of the sunlight, and the people strolling around them at the city walls. For perhaps the first time in his life Parton would be feeling out of touch in some indefinable way with the people among whom he had grown up; he was being made to feel an outsider; and to a man whose life was Tyneside, the unsettling effect would be critical.

'There's one other thing, though,' Parton said suddenly. 'I asked around about this Svensson character a bit more.'

'Did you get anything?' Eric asked quickly.

'A bit. He didn't change much while he was inside; he came back to Tyneside when he got released, and the whisper is he knocked over a store up at Blyth, together with a couple of houses in Gosforth, before things got a bit hot and he scarpered from around here. Talk is he took a freighter to Marseilles. Since then, not a lot.'

'But something?'

'And nothing.' Jackie Parton considered for a moment. 'Good-looking character, this Svensson, that right?'

'He was only seventeen when I nailed him, but yes, burly, dark-haired, well-set-up lad,' Eric admitted.

'Bit of a ladies man, too. At least, the story is he was shacked up with some young girl from Byker when he was sweet seventeen, and the time inside must have sharpened his needs a bit. Anyway, when he came back to the Tyne after his release from Durham, he got involved with the Byker lass again, they say. She's still around.'

'What's her name?'

'She's called Jackson: Cindy Jackson. You think she'll be worth chatting to?'

'You have her address?'

Jackie Parton took out a folded piece of paper from his pocket and handed it to Eric Ward. 'It's on there. I wish you luck with it, but I got a feelin' you're running down a . . . a dead alley.'

He had almost said, a blind alley.

In his darker hours, it was an image that came to Eric Ward himself.

* * *

The office Philip Scarn had chosen as the centre for his business operations on Tyneside was modern, light, airy and commanding a view of the Tyne, curving away to the sea. It was not yet completely furnished, Scarn explained on the Monday morning, but that would be attended to in the next few days. He was delighted that Eric Ward had decided favourably as far as the offer was concerned, and an office on the next floor would be made available for him immediately. In the meanwhile, they could have a preliminary discussion as to the immediate objectives Scarn wished to achieve. First on the legal agenda must be the taking up of two options held on Sunderland sites, and one at Newcastle, on the assumption Eric Ward could clear the change of user application in respect of the Newcastle building.

Eric Ward's mind strayed somewhat as Scarn talked.

The man displayed the same elegant confidence he had demonstrated in London: he was dressed as carefully, this time in a tan suit, and his manner was smooth, confident and superficial as before but as he talked Eric only half listened to what he was saying. It was only when Scarn got around to discussing licensing arrangements that Eric fully concentrated on the conversation. He pointed out that there might be some difficulty in moving at the speed Scarn was contemplating; Scarn's reply was that speed was Ward's problem — that was what he was being paid for, to make use of his contacts.

Eric made use of one of them that very afternoon. He called on Colonel Arkwright, one of the Northumberland justices, and made some enquiries about the licensing scene. He was surprised to find the colonel somewhat evasive; when he made a phone call to another acquaintance on the bench, who had lunched often enough at Sedleigh Hall and held a magistracy in the Sunderland area, he was again aware of a certain reluctance to discuss possible licensing in the town. It was clear that the justices were not happy to talk about night-clubs at the moment; some kind of pressure had been applied in the local political scene, and it was possible that Philip Scarn's plans for the North-East were already more widely known than Scarn himself had realized.

By three in the afternoon Eric was tired and decided he had had enough of the city. He rang Anne's flat in Gosforth to check whether she had come into town and when there was no answer he concluded she had remained at Sedleigh Hall. He called for a taxi to make the drive back to the countryside.

He was in no mood to enjoy the scenery as the taxi took him swiftly northwards. The surgeon had been right: he should try to take things as easily as possible, for the ache was at the back of his eyes again, and while the pain was not as sharp as it had been prior to the operation he had the feeling that the cat claws were still there, just waiting to be extended, to scratch at his eyeballs again and the thought made him shudder. When the car finally swung into the little valley that led to the village and Sedleigh Hall beyond he began to relax, knowing that he would soon be back in the dimness of his bedroom, and able to seek the relief of drugs to alleviate the discomfort he was feeling. As they drew near the drive, however, he was aware of a battered maroon car parked at the grass verge, its nose tilted up against the hedge. Someone was sitting in the driving seat, but Eric was unable to make him out as the taxi flashed past.

Eric paid off the taxi-driver in the courtyard and slowly walked up the steps to the terrace. A fresh breeze from the meadows touched his cheek; the french windows to the sitting-room were open and he stepped inside, feeling grateful for the cool dimness beyond. He called Anne's name, not really expecting that she would be in at this time of day, and then he walked towards the hallway.

She was standing near the foot of the stairs. She seemed frozen, her face pale and her eyes wide and frightened. Her left hand was still resting on the telephone, where she had replaced it in its cradle.

'Anne — what's the matter?' Even as he asked the question, he knew the answer.

She stared vaguely at the phone and then looked up again at Eric. She shook her head slowly, as though the movement would eradicate the memory of what had happened. Then, slowly, she said, 'It . . . it was him.' Eric strode forward and took her by the shoulders; her arms were trembling slightly.

'What did he say?'

'He wouldn't listen . . . he kept talking, saying the same thing. He didn't listen to me, didn't seem to care it was me he was talking to, wouldn't let me interrupt him. It was just—'

'But what did he *say*?'

She stared at Eric, a dark stain of puzzlement and fear spreading in her eyes. 'You must go to the police, Eric.'

'We've already—'

'You *must* go! This man . . . he's mad! He said the same thing, three times, he's going to settle an old score, he's going to kill you, he's waited for years and now it's time! Eric, the police will have to be told—'

'Now just calm yourself down and let's talk about this,' he soothed, even though his body was cold at her words. 'He's a crank; people who make threats over the phone don't carry them out, it's the way they sublimate—'

'But Eric, this man—'

The shrilling of the bell at the front door cut across her words. The sound came like a physical shock; the tension of the moment was increased by the harsh noise and Eric felt Anne's shoulders stiffen under his fingers.

They waited for a few moments and the bell shrilled again, insistently. 'There's no one else in the house,' Anne said, still shaking slightly. 'They've all gone down to the fete in the village. The cook's daughter, she's competing . . .'

Eric left her, walked to the door and opened it.

'Afternoon, squire,' ex-Detective-Inspector Dick Kenton said cheerfully. 'Mind if I come in?'

* * *

The opportunity to be active again, and to undertake a task he was fitted for, seemed to have done wonders for Dick Kenton. He was not now the man Eric had seen shambling in the flat at Keelman's Bridge: his pudgy face seemed ruddier, there was a confident sharpness to his glance, and, shaven, he seemed to have recovered some of the belligerence of earlier days when he had swaggered his way through the Scotswood back streets with Eric Ward in tow. He was dressed in a check shirt that had been newly pressed; his sports jacket was elderly but clean, and his flannel trousers were neat, sharp-edged in their crease. With his hands locked behind his back he strutted now around the sitting-room, inspecting the furniture with approval, taking a deep breath at the windows as he looked out over the terrace and the meadows to the line of the distant Cheviots. He grinned, advanced on Eric and shook his head admiringly. 'You certainly got it set up here, Eric. Lot different from Keelman's Bridge, I'll say that.'

There seemed to be no edge of rancour in his voice, no envy, and yet the admiration in Kenton's tone, with its implications, made Eric irritable. He closed the door, watching Anne walk up the stairs as he did so, then turned back to Kenton. 'I told you that you could phone me—'

'Ah well, thought a visit in person might be a bit better. Give me a chance to look over your set-up as well, of course.' Kenton grinned mischievously. 'Mean to say, not every ex-copper down on his backside gets the chance to end up in a shack like this, is it?'

Eric's irritation increased. A tiny pinpoint of pain lanced at the back of his eyes. He walked towards the terrace, and adjusted his dark glasses against the afternoon sunlight. 'What do you want, Kenton?'

Kenton's tone echoed surprise. 'Well, you did give me a job to do, and I thought—'

'You have something to report?' Eric asked, too quickly.

Kenton watched him for a few seconds, thoughtfully, then scratched his pudgy cheek. 'You awright, Eric?'

'I'm all right.'

'There seemed a kind of funny atmosphere when I came into the hallway. You didn't introduce me to Miss Morcomb . . . You been having a fight? Did I interrupt something—'

'No.' Eric hesitated, then considered there was no reason why Kenton should not know. 'We . . . there's just been another phone call.'

Kenton's head came up; he peered at Eric Ward with interest. 'Same feller? He threaten you again?'

Eric shook his head. 'I didn't take the call; Anne heard him utter the threats. It's all so stupid . . .' He paused, thinking back. 'There was a maroon car near the driveway, someone in it, as I came back to the Hall—'

'That was me,' Kenton said. 'I rang earlier, was told you wouldn't be back till late afternoon, so I drove out anyway, waited down there till you made your appearance-didn't want to burst in on Miss Morcomb when we never been introduced . . .' A slight note of grievance crept into his voice. 'Then I saw the taxi, waited a couple of minutes, and followed you in . . . You got anything to drink here, Eric?'

'There's some whisky and so on over there, in the cabinet. Help yourself.'

He turned aside as Kenton walked over to the cabinet and helped himself to a generous measure of whisky. There was the splash of soda, and a sigh from the ex-detective. 'Ah . . . good stuff, this. But not much of a help—' he paused as he took an appreciative sip at the whisky, 'not if you get threatening phone calls, hey?'

'You implied you had something to report.'

'Aye, well, something and nothing, Eric, something and nothing. Svensson, you said. I been askin' around, old contacts, few new ones, lads from the old days and so on. Funny, it still works, you know, you can still put the arm on villains even though the force is long behind you. It's like they don't forget the old days, and they can't get out from under the old relationship. Aye, I asked around.'

'And what did you hear?'

'Well, that's the funny thing. The story is, Svensson came back to Tyneside when his time was done and indulged in a bit of small-time stuff, breakin' and entering, lock-ups, that sort of thing. But he was pretty clumsy, and things got a bit hot for him — I mean he already had form and the boys in blue ain't fools, are they? So he had to skip. Freighter to Marseilles. Romantic, in a way, don't you reckon?'

'But has he come back again?' Eric asked impatiently.

Kenton was not to be rushed. He took another long sip at his whisky, then waved the glass in a generous gesture. 'Cost me a good bit more than the twenty-five quid you gave me to do the kind of asking around I did, you know. That's one thing: I'll have to learn to put up my charges a bit. Never mind, though. Did Svensson come back to Tyneside? Lemme put it like this. The conventional wisdom says he bought it in Marseilles.'

'He died there?'

'Fished out of the harbour. Got tied in with some little men peddling drugs in a small way. Silly thing to do. The way they got things organized down there, stupid to touch drugs that way. So someone stuck a knife in him, dumped him, and he floated up few weeks later.'

'A few *weeks?*'

Kenton grinned and winked. 'That's the interesting thing, isn't it? Weeks go by. A face gets puffy; the fish have a nibble; putrescence sets in. But he gets *identified*. What was it — papers, teeth, distinguishing marks? For a small-time character like Svensson, they wouldn't take too much trouble, those French coppers. Papers, I reckon, in his pockets — so the morgue, and a file in a cabinet, and forget it all, we got other things on our mind. Don't you reckon?'

Eric Ward stared at him. 'The report is that Svensson is dead, but you're implying—'

'Implyin' nothing, squire. Just listening, picking up facts, surmises . . . You know Svensson had a mother?'

'Everyone has a mother,' Eric said irritably.

'Now there's a thought,' Kenton said, and grinned. 'The funny thing about mothers of villains, though, is that they seem to inspire, sometimes, a kind of . . . even unhealthy respect in their sons. Svensson was like that. Fond of his mother, he was. She died, three weeks ago. Hovel down by the river. Had about three quid set by when she snuffed it. Not much, is it, when you think about it? Bloody Welfare State!'

'I don't understand—'

'Neither do I, squire, neither do I. Mind if I help myself?' Kenton poured himself another drink and then turned back cheerfully to Eric, raising his glass in a toast. 'Here's to Svensson's old lady, though maybe you wouldn't want to join in.'

'What do you mean?'

'Talk is it was her death brought Svensson back to Tyneside.'

'But you said he's *dead!*'

Dick Kenton slipped a hand inside his jacket, ran an appreciative palm over his chest, seeking the muscle that still hardened under the layer of fat that had accumulated of recent years. 'Dorothy bought me this shirt,' he said. 'She's all right . . . can put pride back in a man, you know . . . No, I didn't say Svensson was dead. I said the conventional wisdom holds that he is. But I been talking to more than a few people around the river. And there's a whisper that, dead or not, Svensson's been seen back on Tyneside. Came up from London, recent.' His piggy eyes dwelled on Eric thoughtfully, as he took a stiff drink. '*You* were in London few weeks back, weren't you?'

Eric was silent for a little while. The afternoon sun was slanting long shadows into the room, and a shaft of light picked up the gleam of polish on Dick Kenton's shoes. A sense of pride, returned; Dorothy Farnon was good for him. 'You're suggesting,' Eric said slowly,' that it was someone else got dumped in the harbour at Marseilles, someone with Svensson's papers.'

'It's been done before,' Kenton said indifferently.

'Free of pressures from police and the French underworld, he could then come back to England—'

'To London, where he heard about his mother's death. And then come back to Tyneside.' Something moved slowly in Eric Ward's stomach, a churning, unpleasant feeling. 'If this is the case, if he has returned . . . why should he dredge up an old hate like this, to make threatening calls—'

'Now hold on.' Kenton held up a warning hand. 'We don't know it's Svensson who's making these calls to you. But if it *is*, hell, come on, you don't have to look far for a reason!'

'What reason?'

'Balance, man-or lack of it! You've known enough villains in your time to measure them up! Okay, there's the tearaways, the thickies, the committed, the stupid. All kinds. But there's a hell of a lot of them have one thing in common: a lack of balance, an inability to see facts for what they are. It's always the system that's put them where they are: they believe the stories they tell the probation officers when they're kids. The myths are repeated the first time they're up in court, and after that, it gets ingrained in them. They believe their own hard luck stories. And Svensson? Hell, he's like so many of them. What was he when we nailed him on that roof — seventeen? He'd been lucky up to then, but that night he copped it, with an iron bar, and got a long spell inside. And afterwards, when he comes out, what's he face?'

'He can't hold me responsible—'

'Don't be so bloody naive, Eric! The lad comes out, returns to Tyneside, can't get a job, takes to petty crime again, has to go to France, gets in deep water there — but not the harbour water — and, more cunning now he's older, manages to settle his papers on some stiff who's knifed and dumped. Back to London, a bit of villainy again, maybe — and then his old lady dies. He comes back, he's looking back at how he failed her, didn't care for her when she was old . . . it's all lack of balance, man. Who caught him on that roof? You. Who effectively put him away? You. Who, indirectly maybe, left his mother to die in a slum, because sonny-boy wasn't around to take care of her? You. It was Eric Ward who put Svensson on the slope down. And he wants his own back, now his mother's dead.'

'I can't see it—'

'You think the guy who's phoning you is straight in the head?' Kenton demanded bluntly.

'I don't know. It just seems to me—'

''Course, we don't even know if it is Svensson,' Kenton said easily. 'Just like we don't even know if Svensson is alive. All we *do* know is, someone's giving you the creeps with these phone calls. You and the lass living here, it seems.'

Eric Ward couldn't keep his thoughts along one pathway; the ache in his head had sharpened now, and his vision was becoming blurred. He knew he should have gone straight upstairs for treatment when he arrived, but first the phone call, and then, immediately afterwards, Kenton's arrival had conspired to prevent him going upstairs and to increase the tension under which he was labouring. He took off his glasses, rubbed his eyes hard; the eyeballs were swollen again. He replaced his glasses, took a deep breath, trying to still the quivering nerve ends behind his eyes. 'So what do you suggest?' he asked.

Kenton finished his drink reluctantly, set the glass down and shrugged. 'That's up to you. I been on this a short time. There are other sources I can tap, other people I can see. And there's a few places I can visit, keep an eye on. Cats who return home usually go back to familiar places. Svensson'd be no different. I know his old haunts on Tyneside. I can keep an eye out. But it's up to you, Eric. Maybe Svensson is dead; maybe this is just talk. It'll take time, and patience, to find out. Me . . . I got both.'

For a price, Eric thought wearily. But Kenton could do what he could not. He nodded. 'All right. I'd like you to keep asking around, make further enquiries. I'll pay your expenses, of course — and a fee too.'

'It would help if I could have an advance,' Kenton suggested. 'That twenty-five quid—' .

'I know.' Eric walked across to the table, took out his cheque-book and wrote out a cheque for two hundred pounds. This should see you clear for a while.'

Kenton took the cheque, looked at it silently for a few moments, then slipped it inside his wallet.

'That's pretty generous, Eric.' There was no emotion in his tone. 'I'll do a good job for you. If Svensson is alive, and if he is on Tyneside, I'll find him. And don't worry, I won't con you. We been pals in the past; coppers together. That counts. The moment I'm sure — one way or the other — I'll be in touch. And I guarantee it won't take me more'n two weeks. By then, I'll *know*.'

He pulled his shoulders back as though the cheque in his pocket had further increased his confidence, and Eric was aware that in some respects Dick Kenton had changed but little. The episode at Keelman's Bridge had made him think

Kenton was a broken, failed man; the spring in the man's step now made him realize that Kenton was still tough, hard and, as far as Svensson was concerned, dangerous. Dick Kenton might have begun to grow flabby, but there was still muscle under the fat and he could yet be a match for a man like Svensson, if it ever came to it.

'There's one other thing,' Eric said as he followed Dick Kenton out into the hallway. 'You know much about Johnston O'Connor?'

Kenton stopped, turned to face Eric. A wary note crept into his voice. 'Enough. And perhaps more than I'd like to. What's he got to do with this?'

'Nothing, as far as I know. But he runs the entertainment business in the North, is that right?'

'Most of it. And he's a hard man, Eric.' Kenton paused, eyeing Eric Ward curiously. 'You don't want to go tangling with him. That's a piece of advice you can have free, any time.'

'I'll bear it in mind,' Eric said, and closed the door as Dick Kenton made his way down the steps towards the battered maroon car parked in the gravelled driveway.

* * *

Dawn came the next day with a drizzling rain and a sweeping wind that spattered the window-panes and lifted loose tiles on the roofs of the stables beyond the house. Eric had spent a poor evening and a worse night. Anne's mood had been odd after Dick Kenton had left: she had asked him what Kenton had wanted and only reluctantly had he told her the reason for the man's visit. She had not been pleased when he was forced to admit, finally, that he had asked Kenton to continue making his enquiries among the back streets and pubs of Tyneside.

'Does that mean you're not going to the police?' she demanded. Her eyes had been hot and angry, the red-gold tints in her hair seeming to glow in the evening light.

'There's so little to go on at the moment—'

'That second call gives you plenty to go on! Don't you understand — he threatened to kill you, this time!'

Eric shook his head, took her hand in his and tried to calm her. 'Don't you see, it could just be some crank who will get tired of his silly games in due course? If I go to the police there's so little for them to go on. A somewhat noncommittal phone call—'

'There was nothing noncommittal about the call I heard today! And there was your so-called accident . . . Eric, you're just not taking this thing seriously enough! I'm scared. You must go to the police!'

He had refused. It might have been stubbornness on his part, or it might have been a logical view of the facts at his disposal: he could not be certain. There was the chance that he was motivated by the need not to have her dictate to him — a minor assertion yet again of his independence. He hoped that this was not so, for it was a poor way in which to return her love and the care she had lavished upon him since his time in surgery. But he had refused and she had become withdrawn, and they had spoken little for the rest of the evening.

She did not come to him that night.

He slept badly. In the early, cold hours of the morning when the first soft spattering of rain came down from the Cheviots he lay in his bed, wide awake, staring at the ceiling and seeing again, *feeling* again that night on the roof in Newcastle, when Svensson had faced him with an iron bar. He recalled the scene and yet few of the details: Svensson's face itself was a faded blur. He could remember the man's dark, curling hair, outlined against the glow of light from the fanlight in the flat roof, and he could recall the burliness of the man, young though he had been at the time. Beyond that, there was little, except the crunching of Svensson's broken nose, Dick Kenton leaping up to the roof behind him to help in the arrest. He lay still and there was now only the quick beating of his heart in the darkness, the surge of unreasoning fear in his veins. He tried to think of other things, despairing of sleep, but could not succeed. He thought of Dick Kenton years ago, blustering, bullying, vicious; the awkward scene at Keelman's Bridge and the irony of the situation now, where a man he almost despised might well be the person who would save him from the old hatred that thrust Svensson on to seek revenge.

And he realized, when dawn came after the sleepless night, that he had not told Kenton about Cindy Jackson. Kenton could have visited the girl, to ask her about Svensson. Now, it was something Eric would have to do for himself. The thought pleased him, made him feel actively involved in the solution of his own problems, and he was suddenly glad he had not told the ex-detective-inspector about Svensson's girl-friend in Byker.

* * *

The office in Scarn's premises was furnished already by the time Eric called in later that morning. He spent a few hours checking on the sites that Scarn had mentioned to him and then, during the afternoon, he made a thorough check on the options written into the contracts and the planning applications that were outstanding. One thing was clear: Philip Scarn had been noncommittal at the first meeting about what he intended to do about the kind of entertainment envisaged, but the planning applications and the brief to Eric Ward was straightforward enough. The *entertainment* to be provided was by way of night-clubs and betting shops: Philip Scarn would be throwing down a gauntlet in front of entrenched interests on Tyneside. And that would mean Johnston O'Connor.

That was not Eric Ward's affair. He was being paid, and handsomely, to handle the legal side of things, use his legal expertise and his social contacts. There was no reason why he should look, or worry, further. Nevertheless, he felt uneasy, and wondered whether Scarn knew what he might be letting himself in for.

At five o'clock he left the office and walked to the city centre, raincoat collar turned up against the drizzling rain, head lowered against the curious glances of people who wondered why he wore dark glasses on such an overcast afternoon. He waited among the early evening queues for the bus that would take him out along the Shields Road, and then he sat huddled in the smell of damp clothing as the bus trundled eastwards, over the bridge and into Shields Road, heading for the sprawl of Byker, past Walkergate and, away to his right, the long swing of the Tyne.

He had no idea what to expect; his motives in making this visit were unclear. It was still raining when he got off the bus in the High Street; behind him, as he walked towards the river, was Wallsend and ahead of him the Byker Wall soared, scarring the skyline, twinkling with early lights as people returned home to the rabbit warren of flats buried in the protective wall that had destroyed a community for a roadway that would never be built. He remembered this area from the time he was a boy — he had spent time down at Hunters Quay and watched the ships berthed at the pontoon and dry docks, but so much had changed in twenty years and now it was the wall which dominated everything.

He crossed the wasteland behind the High Street to walk under the archway, and he was in the village that lay in the shadow of the wall itself.

It was a desolate enough place. Some of the terraces remained, a reminder of days gone, but open spaces, scars of muddy ground on which a few elderly cars were parked, gave the only witness to the destruction that had occurred in the re-housing of reluctant families into the Byker Wall itself. He was forced to question a passer-by to obtain directions, disorientated as he was, but a few minutes later he had reached the address given him by Jackie Parton.

It was an island of Edwardian houses, three-storeyed, in a scattering of terraces at the centre of which lay an overblown pub, glittering with fresh paint, incongruous among the decay of the area. The houses were all let out in flats and overlooked the slope that led down through the terraces, past a preserved stretch of Roman wall, to streets named from the glorious, fighting past, commemorating Kitchener and Wilberforce and other Victorian stalwarts. The front garden of the house before which Eric Ward stopped was tiny in size, weed-ridden, stone-flagged, and the front door, when he pushed it open, wheezed and grunted as thought it was now too old to undertake what it was called upon to do.

It was with a feeling of *déjà-vu* that he climbed the stairs: this house was not a world away from Keelman's Bridge though it was at the other end of the city. The odours were familiar, the air of decrepitude similar. And the reluctance of the face behind the door, half-opened to his ring, held echoes of the reluctance he had met in Keelman's Bridge.

It should have been a pretty face, but it was marked with disappointments that had lowered the edges of her mouth and seared it with discontent; the eyes were china blue but held no open innocence, for life on Tyneside had ripped away all innocence and hardened her glance, seeped puffiness into the skin below until she seemed to be looking out of dark wells of suspicion. She might have been blonde when she was sixteen, but her hair was dry, a lifeless yellow that snarled around her thin neck in confused tendrils. Her hand was on the edge of the door, red-painted nails, garish against the dirty brown of the woodwork.

'Are you Cindy Jackson?'

'Who wants to know?' There was a vibrant tinniness about her voice, a light quivering of sound that seemed at odds with her overt personality, vulnerable among the harshness of her skin and hair and eyes.

'My name's Eric Ward.'

'So what do you want with me? I ain't on the game, if that's what yer after.'

'I thought you might be able to help me.'

'With what?'

'Give me answers to a few questions.'

'Like what, for God's sake?'

Eric hesitated. 'Like what happened to a man called Svensson.'

Her eyelids flickered, registering stirrings of alarm, and the red nails contracted against the woodwork, like a cat preparing to leap away in flight. She shook her head, and the tendrils snaked away as she moved to close the door against him. Almost instinctively, the experience and training of the force behind him, Eric leaned against the door, pushing it hard, thrusting the girl inside away and then he was standing in the narrow passageway, and she was yammering at him, nervous, angry, her fingers curling into claws as though she was ready to rend him.

'What the 'ell do you think you're doin'? This is my place and you got no right to come bustin' in here! I been doin' nothing wrong, and if you don't get the 'ell out of here right now I'm going to scream me guts out and you'll be in deeper trouble than you—'

'I just want to ask you a few questions about Svensson.'

Eric stood away from her, not touching her, keeping his voice controlled and calm, unthreatening, and his calmness was suddenly communicated to her. She was smaller than he had realized; her body was plump under the thin dress she wore and she had a good figure. She was perhaps twenty-six years of age, and perhaps she remembered it, as her confidence grew. 'What you say your name was?'

'Eric Ward.'

She stared at him, let the words roll around in her head while she considered them. At last she nodded. 'I know you. Copper.'

'I *used* to be.'

'Recognized you, really. Knew your face . . . but not behind them glasses. You got bad eyes? Been in a fight?'

'Svensson,' he reminded her.

She made no attempt to lead him into the sitting-room beyond the short passageway. 'Funny,' she said. 'The way you remember things even though you think you forgot them, like. I mean, it's years since he was put away. I was a kid, then, but I saw you in court. Heard him shout at you too. Never have thought I'd recognize you, but I did. Spite of those bloody glasses. Got bruises, have you?'

'Where's Svensson now?'

'You used to be a copper,' she said. 'So what you doing now?'

'I'm a solicitor.'

'Just as bad.'

'Svensson,' he insisted.

'Dead,' she said.

They faced each other in the dim light of the passageway. The rain pattered gently on the skylight above their heads and distantly there was the whistle of a boiling kettle. Cindy Jackson raised her chin defiantly and repeated the word. 'Dead'.

'You're sure of that?'

'When a bloke's dead, he's dead.'

'You seen him recently?'

'Are you crazy?' Her eyes flashed suddenly with anger, and for a moment she looked younger and prettier, as though the adrenalin had given her back some of her youth. 'He got killed abroad somewhere, after he left Tyneside.'

'He lived with you, when he came out of prison?'

'That's right.'

'Here?'

'Where else? Now look, Mr Ward, I don't know what the hell this is all about but—'

'I've been told . . . there's a story that he's back on Tyneside.'

Cindy Jackson was silent. Automatically she lifted a hand and twisted her fingers into the yellow tendrils of her hair. She stared at him owlishly. 'What you say?'

'There's a chance he isn't dead. He could be on Tyneside. I wondered if you'd seen him . . . heard from him . . .'

'Christ!' she whispered. 'You must be crazy! He's dead. I heard it. He can't be back around here!'

'If he was, he'd come to see you, wouldn't he?'

She lurched forward, putting her red-nailed fingers on his chest, pushing him backwards into the doorway, grabbing at the woodwork with her free hand. 'You got to get out of here.'

'Please, all I want to know is—'

'You get out. I don't want you in here. I don't want nothin' to do with what's bothering you. I ain't seen him; he's dead, died abroad. I don't want anything to do with him. Now get out. This is my place — you got to get out!'

Her voice had risen, injected with hysteria. There was nothing he could do. He allowed himself to be pushed out on to the landing and the door was slammed in his face. He stood there under the single naked bulb, glowing faintly above him and he waited, but there was no further sound from inside the flat and at last, reluctantly, feeling he had wasted his time coming out here he went back down the stairs, turning up the collar of his raincoat.

He stood in the doorway, peering out into the rain. It was gone six o'clock and the sky was heavily overcast; from behind the tinted glass of his protective spectacles he was unable to make out very much in the street outside.

The wind gusted suddenly and the spattering of rain became a downpour. As the cloudburst darkened the sky the rain tore along the street, blotting out everything as far as Eric was concerned and he huddled back in the doorway, seeking its protection. It was several minutes before the downpour began to slacken and doubtfully he put his head out, peering at the sky, taking off his glasses to do so.

It helped his vision, but only marginally; it was surprising how little he was able to see now, under the dark sky, in the gloom of the street, affected by his own tunnel vision. He stepped out into the street as the rain eased and turned, began to quicken his walk as he moved back towards the hill and the looming mass of Byker Wall. As he did so he was aware of someone else in the street, sheltering in a doorway, like himself.

He had walked for some thirty yards or more before he slowed, hesitant, thinking. Then he stopped, turned, and looked back to the house where Cindy Jackson lived. For several seconds he stood there, indecisively, and then slowly he retraced his steps.

The front door was firmly closed. Eric pressed his hand against it, but it did not move. He moved back into the little garden and raised his head, removing his glasses as rain spattered once more against them. A light gleamed in the window of the flat above, where Cindy Jackson lived. He stared, but there was nothing to see, not even for eyes sharper than his now were. There was a moment when he thought he heard a crashing sound, a woman's voice raised in fear, or anger. But he could not be sure.

Any more than he could be sure that it had been merely a trick of the light, or of memory as he had walked up the street towards the Byker Wall. There had been a man there, sheltering in the doorway: of that he was absolutely sure. Beyond that . . .

He could have been young; he could have been in his mid-twenties. He had been wearing something dark, shiny leather, collar turned up against the rain. Broad shoulders, burly build.

And dark hair.

Faint gleams of light rose in the sky beyond the wall, presaging a lifting of the storm. Eric Ward hurried on, head bent. He did not really want to think about it any more, yet the thoughts came rushing in on him, insistently. The man in the street doorway could have been anyone, a casual passer-by, a man on his way home, sheltering like Eric Ward from the sudden rainstorm. Or it could have been someone else, a man waiting until Eric had left the doorway that led to Cindy Jackson's flat.

A man who knew Cindy Jackson; knew where she lived.

A man called Svensson.

CHAPTER 4

The man who sat facing Eric Ward in the office at police headquarters had unblinking pale blue eyes and an oily skin. His mouth had the precision and conviction of a bigot. His greying hair had been tamed into submission by a stiff brush, and his narrow head seemed oddly placed above the barrel chest under the grey suit. His voice was light, but cold and as he sat his body was taut, leaning forward slightly as though he was always prepared to spring into action. Eric had the feeling the man would be a successful detective, but one in whom the borderline between justified suspicion and paranoid obsession would be a thin one. Once committed, this man would pursue his objective relentlessly. The fact that he might be wrong would rarely, if ever, occur to him.

'We haven't met before, Mr Ward.'

'No.'

'I am Detective-Superintendent Bateman.'

'I'm pleased to meet you,' Eric said, but wasn't.

'Yes. We've never met, but I've heard about you.' Bateman's pale eyes flickered over Eric as though testing the reality of sight against the theory of gossip. 'You spent some time with the force, before my arrival.'

'That's correct.'

Bateman placed his hands on the desk in from of him and gazed at them dispassionately. The fingers were slim and predatory: he appeared to be proud of them. 'The records would imply that your . . . career in the force was an exemplary one; you had a reasonable success rate and your files disclose that you were highly regarded. It was a pity, the circumstances of your release. Glaucoma.'

That's right,' Eric said woodenly.

'Particularly painful, I understand, and certainly debilitating. And then you turned to the profession of the law, having taken the sensible precaution of taking a law degree while you were still with the force. You demonstrated foresight in that . . . even if your career with Francis, Shaw and Elder was relatively short.'

'We had differences.'

'Quite so. But now you have a new job.'

'That's right.'

'Is that wise? So soon after your operation?'

Bateman was watching him carefully, narrow head tilted as though to hear his answers better, his attitude nevertheless remote, a scientist observing a specimen. Eric had the impression that the questions had been mechanical, an exercise in which the words were designed merely to give the man time to observe, visually dissect the man facing him. Eric disliked the feeling. 'The decision wise or not, was mine and has been taken.'

'Quite so. And the job you have, it's working for Philip Scarn, isn't it?'

Eric took a deep breath. 'Look, let's stop this aimless chatting; I've better things to do than sit here discussing matters that are personal to me. I received a phone call at my office, a polite request to call to see you here at headquarters. All right, I'm here. Now what is it you want to see me about?'

Bateman's face was unnaturally calm but his eyes narrowed like a cat's. 'I think it's for you to tell me, really, Mr Ward.'

'What do you mean?'

'I am acting in response to a phone call from your . . . friend.' The word was stained in his mouth; he did not like it himself and his dislike and disapproval was communicated to Eric. 'It would seem she has acquaintances who are able to exercise some pressure, in addition. Normally, as you would know, an officer of my seniority would not deal with such a . . . trivial complaint.' He gazed at his hands again. 'On the other hand, since you are an ex-member of this force—'

'Miss Morcomb reported the matter to you?' Eric asked stiffly.

'Not to me *personally*, but the Chief Constable has landed it on my desk.'

'I told her not to make such a report.'

'The extent to which you control Miss Morcomb's actions is your affair and of no consequence at this time. The fact is, she has made a report, influence elsewhere has dictated the Chief Constable himself should be involved, and he has asked me to handle it. I too have better things to do, Mr Ward, but the file lies on my desk. So perhaps we can deal with it as quickly as possible. As I understand it, you have been in receipt of threatening phone calls.'

'Two.'

'Both taken by you?'

'Only the first. The second — which was more explicit than the first-was taken by Miss Morcomb.'

'And she is understandably alarmed.' Bateman permitted a thin smile to touch his lips. 'But you . . . ?'

'I . . . discounted it at first. But then, in view of my accident—'

'Ah yes, the fall in London. But it *was* an accident, wasn't it?'

'I thought so at the time.'

'But the phone calls made you revise your opinion. I see. Not very much to go on, is there? Hysteria can come easily to a woman.'

'Now look—'

'Do you have any idea who might be making these calls?' Bateman interrupted smoothly.

Eric hesitated. 'I'm not sure. There were three possibilities that occurred to me: two of them, on investigation, I decided can be ruled out. The third, well, I'm not yet certain.'

'And his name?'

'Svensson.'

'Ah yes.' The slim fingers strayed to the manila folder on the desk, picked at its edge and then reluctantly opened the file. It held a single sheet of paper, closely typewritten. Bateman leaned forward, inspecting the sheet. He nodded slowly. 'Yes. Svensson. Joseph Svensson, died on or about March 30th 1980, Marseilles. Cause of death, knife wound, the blow administered slightly from behind and to the left, suggesting a left-handed killer. Problems of identification because of three-week immersion in the harbour overcome by various details: clothing, personal possessions, recent movements of the deceased. And the fact he had been under surveillance by the French police. Drug offences, small-time. A gangland killing, Mr Ward, and the police had better things to do there, too. So . . .'

'Svensson—'

'Is dead, Mr Ward.'

The mouth shut like an iron trap on the words, brooking no dispute. Eric stared at the detective-superintendent, surprised at the man's sharpness. He shrugged. 'All right, if that's true, there's still someone making these calls and I'll have to look elsewhere.'

'Yes. You used the word *investigation* earlier, didn't you? But now you — or your friend — have involved us, there's little need for you to investigate further, is there? We'll make any necessary enquiries now on your behalf.' The slim fingers closed the file, smoothing the cover gently. 'You can leave it with us.'

'And Svensson—'

'I have explained. He died in Marseilles.'

Recklessly, eager to shock the controlled man facing him, Eric burst out, 'Then how do you also explain that he has been seen in London, that rumour has it he's come back to Tyneside?'

'Rumour only,' Bateman said complacently.

'And if I tell you I think I've seen him myself?'

'Where?'

'Outside the flat belonging to his ex-girl-friend.'

The pale blue eyes were now fixed on Eric with an odd intensity. The iron-hard mouth moved, testing the words. 'His ex-girl-friend, she is called . . .'

'Cindy Jackson.'

The room was silent. Something had retreated in Bateman's face, like a cat backing into a corner, facing the danger of a menacing dog. His eyes had glazed over, as though turning inside reflectively and the lips were pursed again, meanly, tightening on the truth. From another room there came the rattle of coffee cups; from beyond the window a distant rumble of lorries making their way north. Inside the interview room the clock ticked loudly. Bateman stirred, and put his hands below the desktop.

'I think, Mr Ward, you're making a mistake.' His tone suggested it was a *bad* mistake.

In a level, controlled tone, Eric said, 'I can't be sure, of course. It was raining, my eyesight is affected, but there was a man waiting outside Cindy Jackson's flat while I was in there. He was standing in a doorway—'

'Merely a passer-by, sheltering from the rain.'

'He was burly, dark-haired; it *could* have been Svensson.'

'Hardly.'

'I'm certain he entered the flat after I left. The front door was firmly closed when I returned; I heard voices, some sort of commotion from her flat—'

'Mr Ward.' The interruption was delivered icily. 'I won't say it again. Svensson is dead. When Miss Morcomb phoned in she mentioned the name; the Chief Constable asked me to check it out; I have already been to a considerable amount of trouble to do just that. The information we have from Marseilles is quite definite: the identification is complete. The man you suspect has been phoning you is *dead*. Some other crank is involved. That means two things. First, your own *investigations* have proved amateur and abortive — they can cease right now. The matter lies with us and we'll see to it. Second, since Svensson is no longer in the land of the living there is no need for you to go around bothering innocent people.'

'Cindy Jackson—'

'Can in no manner be involved in your troubles. Stay away from her. I would be extremely sympathetic towards her were she to seek help in stopping you bothering her.' His pale eyes held Eric's challengingly. 'I mean what I say, Mr Ward. We'll do all we can to help you clear up this business of the phone calls, but we can't have you running around bothering people. So, stop your own investigations, leave it to us — and stay away from Cindy Jackson.'

'Is that all?' Eric Ward asked coldly, rising to his feet.

'Not quite.' Bateman rose too, standing heavy and solid on his feet, his eyes not shifting but the bright glare becoming more intense. 'Just a piece of advice, really. Are you *sure* you're fit enough to be working so soon after your operation?'

Eric wasn't, but deemed that none of Bateman's business.

'It just seems to me,' Bateman continued, 'that you would be more sensible considering your health, long term, than rushing into employment with Philip Seam. The job he's given you . . . it could involve a certain strain.'

'You seem very interested — and very knowledgeable about my job with Scarn.'

'News gets around,' Bateman replied noncommittally. 'This is only advice, of course, but I think you should reconsider this employment. Good day, Mr Ward.'

Eric left the headquarters thoughtfully. Something odd was going on, something was out of tune, jarring in the conversation. But it was not until later that evening, when he spoke to Anne, that he was able to define what it was. When he told her he had been called to police headquarters she was immediately defensive, but defiant too. It had been for his own good; he was foolish to leave the matter to Parton and Kenton; the police needed to be informed when threats of this kind were being made.

'When you phoned the police,' Eric asked, 'who did you speak to?'

'A detective called Jenkins.'

'Ahuh . . . Freddie Jenkins, I know him. And after that?'

She was puzzled; a small frown appeared on her brow. 'What do you mean?'

'Did you speak to anyone else at headquarters?'

'No. Jenkins said he would deal with it.'

Eric stared at her, thoughtfully. 'He isn't dealing with it. A super called Bateman has taken it over.'

'So?'

'So who else did you speak to? Outside headquarters.'

'I don't know what you're talking about. I just made the one call; Jenkins took it; he said he'd deal with it; I raised it with no one else at all.'

'None of your county friends . . . none of the magistracy?'

She was silent for a moment, staring at him, and then she shook her head, making no reply. Instead she asked him, 'What's this about, Eric?'

He sipped his coffee, and shook his head in turn. 'I don't know. A small enough matter — threatening phone calls. It might normally have been put down to a woman's hysteria; they'd have sent a constable round to have a chat. Instead, Jenkins put it upstairs, the Chief Constable handed the file to a senior officer.'

'There!' Anne exclaimed triumphantly. 'At least *they're* taking it seriously.'

Too seriously, Eric thought, but did not say so aloud.

He was puzzled. The Chief Constable didn't normally get involved in such matters personally, nor would he normally delegate the task to one of his senior detectives. Ann had mentioned the name Svensson to them over the phone, and it had caused enough of a flurry for them to contact, apparently, the French police.

Yes, they were taking it seriously.

Equally serious had been Detective-Superintendent Bateman's warning. They wanted Eric to stop his own nosing around, and they wanted him to stop bothering Cindy Jackson. He could hardly tell Bateman at the time that since seeing the man he believed to be Svensson outside Cindy's flat he had taken steps to get more information. And he had no intention of reversing his track just because Bateman was ordering him to do so.

Jackie Parton had the matter already in hand.

* * *

At two in the morning it was time for Jackie Parton to be relieved. He had made arrangements with an old friend and drinking companion, Fred Long, to take over from him, to keep watch on Cindy Jackson's flat. No one had gone in or out since ten that evening, when Cindy had returned, somewhat the worse for wear it seemed after a session at the Black Horse, and the street had been quiet since twelve. He was glad when Fred turned up at ten minutes past the hour: he had feared the man had forgotten.

'Twenty quid's worth twenty quid,' Fred Long muttered, grinning in the darkness. 'Everything all quiet?'

'As the grave. But I'm frozen,' Parton growled. 'Be back about six, all right?'

Neither of them noticed the man in the shadows at the end of the back lane; dressed in a dark leather jacket he was difficult to spot, particularly since he was taking every opportunity to remain unseen. When Parton walked away, back down the street, he did not see him, and the first intimation Fred Long had that there was anyone at all in the vicinity was when an arm snaked around his neck from behind, he took a vicious blow in the kidneys and half fell, to be dragged downwards into the darkness of the back lane. A foot took him heavily on the head and as lights crackled and exploded in his brain he lost consciousness, unaware of the boot being driven systematically and with increasing violence into his ribcage.

Several minutes later, Cindy Jackson heard the key turn in the lock . . . She was instantly awake, coming out of a light, drink-induced doze. She got up from the settee where she had collapsed once she returned at ten and scratched her head. She heard the door close and she yawned, turned towards the door as it opened.

'Hey, bonny lad,' Cindy breathed, rubbing her finger against her nose sleepily. 'I thought you'd never come back—'

The words died on her lips.

* * *

The morning clientele at the Hydraulic Engine were subdued and not merely by Eric Ward's presence. There was evidence of there having been a riotous night at the pub during the previous evening: stale beer and stale smoke still stained the atmosphere, a rickety piano had been brought into the bar and not removed, and the floor was still littered with confetti. One of the local Irishmen had decided to get married, it seemed, and his friends had treated the occasion as an Irish wake. One young man was still sleeping In the corner. The barman did not seem to mind: presumably the profits of the evening's entertainment had been enough to allow him to overlook such aberrations.

Eric had to wait for twenty minutes before Jackie Parton kept his appointment. The meeting was the result of a short, direct conversation on the phone at seven that morning. Parton had used no preliminaries: he wanted to see Ward at eleven-thirty. There had been no explanation. Now, when Parton finally arrived, he cast one glance in Eric's direction, ordered a pint for himself and then stayed at the bar, drinking it purposely. Eric considered joining him at the bar, but thought better of it: there was something about the set of the ex-Jockey's shoulders that suggested Jackie Parton wanted no one's company but his own at that point in time. He waited patiently, with his glass of orange juice, feeling the first prickling of a subdued anxiety behind his eyes. At last Parton finished his pint, collected another, and came across to join Eric in the window-seat.

He was silent for a while. His eyes were hooded, and he fingered the break in his nose reflectively, as though recalling old pains. Then his twisted lip lifted sourly, and he said, 'Don't think you been square with me, Mr Ward .'

Eric stared at him silently for several seconds. 'What's happened?'

'I think you always had more information than you was prepared to give me. You been playin' things close to your chest I can understand that, loyalty to a client and all that, 'it's big with a solicitor, ain't it? But same time, if you use a feller, get him to work for you, there's loyalty due there too, isn't that right? So you should have been straighter with me, Mr Ward. Put me in the picture.'

'*What's happened?*'

'I got a marrer: Fred Long. Known him a long time, we was stable boys together. He never made the big time the way I did, and a couple of bad rides finished him in the 'sixties. But he's all right, I was always a mucker of his, and when I had a job to do I used to use him as back-up. Like last night.'

'And?'

'He's in hospital this morning. He got worked over last night. Very efficiently.'

'What the hell are you talking about?'

Jackie Parton's eyes glittered and his mouth twisted unpleasantly. 'Can't put it any simpler, Mr Ward. I found Fred in the back lane at six this morning. He wasn't a pretty sight. He was moaning, bleedin' from the mouth and nose. Side of his head had taken a boot and he got several ribs smashed, seems like. He was breathing bad. I got him to hospital, and I phoned you. Then I waited a while, made a few phone calls — and suddenly a few whispers got through to me at last. You should've told me, Mr Ward, not leave me set up like that. It could have been me, last night. And Fred's me marrer. And there's nothing I can do about it.'

'Jackie, I've no idea what you're talking about.'

It was as though there was a glass wall between them: Jackie Parton heard the words, but did not believe them. When he spoke, his voice was thin and dry, curiously attenuated. 'It's no good, Mr Ward. The whisper's out. You're working for Scarn and the only reason Scarn's come back north is to put the needle into Johnston O'Connor. That's what the entertainment kick is about isn't it? Scarn's not after making a profit — he just wants to put the skids under O'Connor. I had the bloody feeling in my bones, right from the beginning.'

'I swear to you—'

'Don't say nothing like that; cuts no ice. A lawyer'll swear his grandmother away. But I thought you was different; I thought we could trust each other.'

Eric Ward leaned forward, gripped Jackie Parton's arm in a fierce grip. 'Listen to me. I don't know what the hell you're talking about. I asked you to keep an eye on Cindy Jackson's flat for one reason only — to discover whether Svensson is back on Tyneside and living with her, visiting her. That's all. This business about Philip Seam, you've got me confused—'

'You talking straight with me?' Suspicion still stained Parton's voice. 'You really don't know anything more'n you've told me?'

'It's the truth, Jackie.'

The calmness of his tone carried conviction to the ex-jockey. Some of the anger left Parton's eyes and he fingered his scarred lip thoughtfully. After a while, he mumbled, 'Maybe I went off a bit at half-cock. Seein' Fred like that, it churned me.'

Eric rose, went up to the bar and ordered the little man another pint of brown ale, got another orange juice for himself and walked back to the table. The ex-jockey had finished his second drink, and reached at once for the one placed in front of him by Eric Ward. 'No reason why I don't take on a skinful today,' he muttered.

'After you've told me all you've heard,' Eric said quietly.

Parton looked at him across the glass of beer. He shook his narrow head. 'Heard . . . or not heard. I can't get the straight of it, Mr Ward, but there's odd things going on. You remember, I told you one time no one was saying anything: contacts had clammed up? Well, not now, not all the way. But what's coming out is kind of garbled. First off, can you tell me the connection between your character Scarn and Cindy Jackson?'

'I've no idea.'

'Neither do I . . . but the whisper is, there is one. Second, your name is around: it's common knowledge you're working for Scarn, and I think maybe that's why Fred got clobbered last night. Teach him — and me — a lesson. You and your employer, you're bad news among some of the Tyneside wild boys. Them who's got contacts with O'Connor.'

'I don't understand—'

'There's more. The *fuzz* is also interested in Cindy Jackson.'

'The police?' Eric was about to say more, and then recalled the curious attitude displayed by Detective-Superintendent Bateman; that, and the man's involvement, as well as the Chief Constable's interest. He looked at Jackie Parton. 'Just what is going on, Jackie?'

'You tell me.'

'I've been warned off, at police headquarters. Warned off going to see, or bother, Cindy Jackson.'

'Then take the advice,' Parton said feelingly. 'If O'Connor *and* the police are saying the same thing to you, listen to them! I intend to take the hint! End of the line for me, Mr Ward.'

'But what about Svensson?'

Jackie Parton stared at him for several seconds, then shook his head slowly. 'Sorry, but I can't help. The story I hear is, he's dead. I think you'd better leave it like that.'

'And the phone calls?'

Jackie Parton shrugged. 'I think maybe you're barking up the wrong tree. These characters — O'Connor's boys — if you've been treading on their toes by helping Philip Scarn, maybe it's their way of scaring you off. But I reckon you needn't take it too seriously — not if you break with Scarn. He's the key to the whole thing.'

Eric Ward wasn't so sure. He offered no argument, but the sequence was wrong for it to have been the action of a Tyneside mob leader. The push down the steps at King's Cross, if it had *not* been an accident, had come too soon for it to have been the work of one of O'Connor's men; similarly, the first threatening phone call had occurred before he had agreed to work for Philip Scarn.

Nevertheless, Jackie Parton was right. The key to the puzzle lay with Philip Scarn.

The bar had suddenly fallen silent. There was the buzz of a trapped fly at the window-pane: it was the loudest sound in the room. Jackie Parton did not turn his head; he kept his head down, staring at his beer, but there was something in his face that betrayed a certain tension, as though he guessed what might have happened, had indeed dreaded the possibility without speaking of it. Eric Ward turned his head and looked across to the doorway. A man stood there, tall, in uniform.

He came across and he was polite, courteous, and firm. 'Mr Eric Ward?'

He was a young constable, no one Eric knew. 'Yes, that's right.'

'I was told you had an appointment here. I wonder if you'd mind accompanying me?'

'Where?'

'You'll see when we get there, sir.'

'I'd still like to—'

'It's Detective-Superintendent Bateman, Sir. He'd like to have a word with you.'

The room was still and silent as Eric Ward followed the young constable out to the car.

* * *

Bateman's oily skin was pale with suppressed anger as he stared at Eric Ward. The mouth was twisted like bent iron, and a pulse beat in his throat, thrusting irritability through his veins in a steady, angry throbbing. Eric Ward felt cold. He had expected the car to take him from the Hydraulic Engine to police headquarters: instead, it had cut up into Elswick Road and sped across the city to pick up the short stretch of motorway that led to the coast. His heart had begun to sink then, and he remembered the look on Jackie Parton's face. The police car raced into Shields Road, over Byker Bridge, and as the Byker Wall loomed up Eric knew that Parton had guessed the trouble that had occurred last night had not been restricted to outside the flat. The confirmation was complete when the car stopped outside Cindy Jackson's flat.

Bateman had been standing at the top of the stairs, flanked by two uniformed men as Eric came up to meet him. There was a flurry of men inside the flat, and Eric caught a glimpse of a shell, lying in the passageway, waiting to be used.

Bateman glared at him, his cold pale eyes vicious. 'You'd better come in, Ward. I thought you'd better have a look at her, before they take her away.'

He led the way into the dingy sitting-room. The settee was lying on its side, its guts spilling out over the threadbare carpet, flock and padding displaying its age in a world of plastic foam. A table lamp had been smashed, but apart from these two items there seemed to have been little disturbance. The attack had been clinically executed, deliberate and precise. But there must have been unnecessary anger there, too.

The girl lay on her back. Her mouth had been split open, and blood had begun to congeal in her ear. Her eyes were bruised, her blouse torn and red marks stained the whiteness of her breast. 'She was punched,' Bateman said coldly, 'and kicked. Maybe they talked a while, but it wouldn't have been for long. He laid into her, slammed the hell out of her, and then he walked out. He left her, she was still alive. But some time during the night, the lab will be able to tell us in due course, she choked, swallowed her own blood. From her records down at headquarters, she'd have been twenty-four in about three weeks' time.'

They were bringing the shell into the room; the photographer had finished and the plastic sheet was being unrolled carefully. Detective-Superintendent Bateman turned to Eric Ward and in a sudden spurt of viciousness snarled, 'Well, are you satisfied now? Didn't I tell you to stay the hell away from this girl?'

* * *

He had neither wanted nor expected to visit Keelman's Bridge again.

Oddly enough it was not as gloomy an experience as he had anticipated. As he crossed the Scotswood Bridge the Tyne seemed to sparkle under the hot afternoon sun and ahead of him the folds of the Durham hills were a soft green, lush against the intense blue of the sky. The recent rain had washed the air and the streets seemed cleaner, less grimy.

When he climbed the stairs to the flat the stale odours seemed to have been eradicated and the stairs themselves were not as ill-lit as he remembered. He rang the bell and this time there was no shuffling, no peering around the door by an ill-shaven Dick Kenton. Instead, Dorothy Farnon stood there, dressed in a neat skirt and short-sleeved jumper, well-groomed, either just about to go out, or just returned to the flat.

'Mr Ward!'

'Is Dick here?'

She hesitated, staring at him as though she were weighing something up in her mind, then nodded. 'You'd better come in.'

He followed her into the sitting-room and it was not as seedy as he remembered. Dorothy Farnon had cleaned the room recently: the furniture, he recalled had been serviceable but lacking in real comfort; now there was a small new coffee table and in the corner by the window a shining new music centre comprising radio, record player and recording facilities. Dorothy Farnon saw him staring at it and with a certain defensiveness in her tone said, 'If we have to stay in during the evenings there's no need to watch the rubbish on the telly all the time, is there? I had a bit of money put aside, I didn't tell Dick about it, but now he's . . . active again, and things are settling better, I thought I might as well spend the little I had, treat ourselves a bit, make the flat a bit more cosy, like.' Her eyes narrowed slightly. 'Not so well set up as you, but no reason why we shouldn't be comfortable, is there?'

He had the vague feeling she regretted the words even as she spoke them, but they had tumbled out with a hint of envy before she could restrain them. Now she stared at him, slightly annoyed with herself, slightly embarrassed. She wore less make-up today and oddly enough it made her look younger so that he could remember the woman he had known years ago. Perhaps something of the thought was exposed in his face for her glance dropped. 'Dick's out at the moment — I'm expecting him back shortly.'

'Oh. Well, look, I can—'

'You don't look well.' There was a surprising sharpness in her tone, and her glance was clinical again, weighing him up. 'Are you all right?'

Eric brushed the question aside irritably. 'It's nothing; I'm just a bit tired, that's all.'

'You look as though you've had a rough time.' She hesitated, then turned towards the kitchen. 'Sit down. I'll get you a beer.'

Eric Ward did as he was told. He sat down. She was right. He had had a rough time; the worse, because he had been made to feel responsibility for a girl's death.

* * *

Detective-Superintendent Bateman's anger had been controlled but vicious. It was as though he was taking the death of Cindy Jackson personally; it may have been that he felt there had been action he could have taken which would have avoided it. If so, he was determined to slough off any such feeling of responsibility on to Eric Ward. Back at police headquarters he had made Eric sit down in front of him in the interview room while he railed at him for several minutes, stressing the fact that Eric had been ordered not to interfere, had been told to keep his nose out of police affairs, had been instructed to stay away from the girl, but all the time the attack was delivered in precise, sharp sentences, marked only by a cold anger, the worse for its icy control.

Finally, Eric's own anger broke through. 'Now hold on, Bateman! You've had your say, now let me have mine! Just why you should assume the girl's death is in any way connected with me I can't imagine, and why the hell you've thought it necessary to drag me up there to confront me—'

'I've had a report,' Bateman cut in, 'of the hospitalization of a man called Alfred Long. He was taken to the hospital this morning by a friend of yours: Jackie Parton. It takes no great leap of the imagination to reach the conclusion that Long was beaten up outside the flat — Parton will be making a statement to us right now. But you were instructed to stay away. Instead, you deliberately chose to disobey that instruction, you set this man Long to watch the flat, and I want to know why!'

'All right, all right,' Eric said irritably as the old familiar ache began behind his eyes. 'I asked Parton and he used Fred Long to help — to watch the flat. But the arrangement was made before you talked to me, and I saw no reason to stop it.'

'No reason?'

'I wanted to find out if Svensson was staying with her; if he had really returned to Tyneside; if he was the man making the calls to me.'

Bateman's cold eyes seemed to glow. 'Svensson is dead. I've told you. That story cuts no ice with me, Ward. I want to know just what you're playing at. What the hell you're doing, fronting for Scarn this way.'

'Scarn?' Eric Ward took off his tinted glasses and rubbed his fingers over his eyeballs, lids tight shut against the growing pain. 'What the hell has Scarn got to do with Cindy Jackson?'

'Why don't *you* tell *me*?'

Eric shook his head desperately. 'I haven't a clue what you're on about. Svensson—'

'To hell with Svensson! I want the truth, Ward! You were told to set a watch on the girl because Scarn had picked up some information. We want to know—'

Eric Ward stood up violently. The chair turned over behind him as the lancing pain caused him to explode in frustration and anger. 'I don't know what the hell you're talking about! I've already told you why I was watching Cindy Jackson — if you don't like the story I tell, you know what you can do with it! This rubbish about Scarn goes straight over my head. I'm employed by him to do his legal work. That's all.'

'Legal work, dirty work,' Bateman said, contempt staining his tone. 'I suppose you'll now be telling me that you've never even heard of a man called Paddy Reilly?'

'Who the hell is he supposed to be?'

'Another of Cindy Jackson's boy-friends,' Bateman said in a surge of anger, 'and the one we know was responsible for the beating she got here last night!'

Something happened to Detective-Superintendent Bateman's face as soon as the· words were out. He clearly regretted saying them. His mouth twisted in sudden annoyance, his angry eyes became hooded and Eric knew that the man was annoyed with himself for saying more than he had intended. The annoyance spilled over, directed towards Eric Ward. 'I tell you, Ward,' Bateman said in a vicious tone, 'you're the kind who causes more trouble than he's worth! All right, you had a sound reputation in the force and kept your nose clean, but you cried your heart out when you left with that bloody ailment of yours, and you've been crying ever since. Oh, sure, we all know you got qualified, became a bloody solicitor, but it was never really enough, was it? I've heard about that Egan business a few years' back: you had to meddle there, didn't you? Almost got yourself killed, too damned pity you didn't! And then there was the Saxby business: it seems to me you didn't exactly come out of that affair smelling of roses, did you? Well, let me tell you this: you're dealing with someone else in this particular situation, and Detective-Superintendent Bateman just doesn't intend to see you messing about in police investigations. If you want to get involved with shady business operations, that's entirely your affair, but the moment you step out of line, and start blocking police business again, I'll get you drummed out of Tyneside, so damned hot that no legal office will ever employ you again! Sail close to the wind, my friend and I'll have you blacked by the Law Society! If you hadn't stuck your bloody nose in, if you hadn't been sniffing around Cindy Jackson's skirts, she wouldn't be dead right now! *Remember* that! Now get the hell out of this office — and remember: stay out of my way!'

* * *

Dorothy Farnon walked across to the record player, placed a disc on the turntable, switched it on, and a few seconds later the first of Streisand's *Love Songs* filtered through to Eric's consciousness. The music was low and soft; it soothed him, and he pressed the cold glass of lager against his forehead. In a while he began to feel better, some of the pain caused by the nervous tension beginning to fade. He opened his eyes. Dorothy Farnon was sitting opposite him, a glass of beer in her hand, watching him. It was not sympathy in her glance so much as calculation. Maybe she thought he might inconveniently die in her sitting-room. She'd had troubles enough.

'Feeling better now?' she asked flatly.

'I'm all right, thanks. Sorry if I—'

'You were looking rough. Been overdoing it, right?'

'Something like that.'

'Want to talk about it?' She watched him, like a building society manager concerned about his deposit, leaning forward slightly, black hair framing her pale face, eyes marked with a calculating concern. She had lived with one policeman who had been killed, and lived now with another who had been forced to retire. Perhaps some of their professional drive had rubbed off on her. 'Talking about things can help, sometimes.'

He shook his head, leaned back in the easy chair. 'No. I'll be fine in a moment. The music, and the beer . . .'

She nodded, a little disappointed, and sat back herself. The music moved softly around them, until suddenly Dorothy Farnon sat up jerkily. 'That'll be Dick,' she announced.

Her hearing was more finely attuned than Eric's, for he had not heard the key in the lock. Or maybe she had been listening more carefully for the sound than he had. She was rising, walking quickly towards the passageway, to greet Dick Kenton. Eric sat with his head back, waiting. He heard her voice, low, the words indistinguishable, as she spoke to Dick Kenton. Eric could guess she would be warning him of Eric's presence, and his state. It didn't matter.

Had he *really* been responsible for Cindy Jackson's death?

Dick Kenton was standing in front of him, burly, solid, and concerned. 'You feelin' all right, Eric?'

'Dorothy's revived me well, the beer, the music.'

'Okay.' Dick Kenton still stood there uncertainly, peering at Eric with a trace of anxiety in his eyes. He looked tired, and somehow shabbier than the last occasion Eric had seen him. He was wearing an old pair of grubby twill trousers and his jacket had seen better days, the arms and shoulders grimy, one elbow stained with an oily mark. He turned to Dorothy. 'I'll have a beer too, luv.' He ran a hand over his mouth, as though the thought of the beer reminded him he was thirsty. Eric noticed his fingernails were broken and dirty. Some of the sense of pride in appearance that had returned to Dick Kenton seemed now to have deserted him again. Or maybe he had been specially spruced up for his visit to Sedleigh Hall.

'So what's the problem, lad?'

Eric was suddenly confused, not certain what he was doing here with Kenton. His disorientation might be due to his uncertain health, the latent, constant fear of the pain that could strike, the tension aligned to his tunnel vision, but it was real enough and the events of the last twenty-four hours had served to damage his logic, render him incapable of fully rational thought. Jackie Parton, Bateman, Cindy Jackson, Philip Scarn, somehow they were now all inextricably linked in a riddle that was beyond his unravelling.

'Reilly,' he said, the word blurting out almost in a panic. 'Paddy Reilly. You ever heard of him?'

Dick Kenton's eyes were blurred with surprise. It was not a question he had been expecting; now, he waited, thinking, until Dorothy Farnon came in and placed a can of beer in his hand. He took a long draught; she stood just behind him, watching them both, a hint of nervousness in her stance. Kenton belched softly, then repeated the name. 'Paddy Reilly. Aye, man, I've heard of him. But what's he to do with you?'

'Who is he?'

'I'm surprised you don't remember him. Young tearaway he was, before he saw sense. Borstal, when he hammered an old man in a mugging down at Pink Lane. We hauled him in couple of times after that . . . but maybe it was about that time you was down at Hendon.' Kenton was unable to keep the trace of an old rancour out of his voice, a bitterness that he had never been chosen to attend the police training school. It was all in the past, but some things a man never came to terms with, Eric thought.

'I don't remember him,' Eric said. 'What happened to him?'

'He's still around, but bigger and, on the surface, cleaner.' Dick Kenton took another thoughtful sip at his can of beer. 'He's bigger, in the sense that he don't do his own rough-housing now, can pay lads to do it for him. And cleaner, in that he works behind legitimate fronts, even if the money comes from dirt. But there's one way he'd never change.'

'What's that?'

'Temper. Uncontrollable, when he's riled. In the right situation he'd still be capable of putting the boot in.'

Eric watched the ex-detective standing in front of him. He did not really see him, however, for his thoughts had strayed back to the flat in Byker, and Cindy Jackson, sprawled in her blood on the floor. Kenton seemed momentarily confused under Eric's unseeing scrutiny and reached for the other chair, pulled it forward, sat down. Eric pulled himself together. 'Did you know that this man Reilly had been a lover of Cindy Jackson's?'

'Who's Cindy Jackson?'

Eric was surprised: he had assumed Tyneside gossip would have reached Kenton. 'She used to be Svensson's girl, at the time he was arrested.'

'Hell's flames,' Kenton said wonderingly, after a short silence. 'I remember her now . . . she was in court. Nice kid. She was a . . . she was a clerk or something, I recall. At the time I wondered what she was doing, tied in with a tearaway like Svensson. But Paddy Reilly — that would explain it. She was just plain gullible, plain stupid.'

'How do you mean?'

Kenton grinned unpleasantly. 'I told you Reilly's money was dirty. It's *very* dirty. He's got the agency for the red light area: he runs the girls for Johnston O'Connor.'

'O'Connor again!'

'Aw, come on, Eric, you must know O'Connor's taken over most of the shady business in Newcastle these last few years. Reilly's served him for some time back, and has been given his slice of the action. And his best talents were in the girls' direction. He started by recruiting them himself. Handsome bastard; always was. Big lad; strong. Jet-black curly hair. Oh aye, if the story is this lass was his girl-friend, believe me, the way it would be is after Svensson went inside, Reilly would have recruited her — and kept his hooks in her. That'll be the way of it. And I'll bet my last quid that she'll have given up office work long ago.'

'She's dead,' Eric said dully.

Kenton exploded into a brief obscenity. He took another drink, turning over the information in his head. In the background Dorothy Farnon moved restlessly, and Kenton looked at her briefly, before turning back to Eric. 'This girl . . . she's dead. How do you—'

'I was pulled in by the police. Detective-Superintendent Bateman, no less.'

'What the hell for?'

'He considers I . . . precipitated the killing.'

'How, for God's sake?'

Eric sighed, shook his head helplessly. 'I don't know; I just can't think straight. Bateman seems to think there's some connection between me, my employment with Philip Scarn, and the death of Cindy Jackson. I'll have to sort it out with Scarn, but—'

Dick Kenton glanced quickly again at Dorothy Farnon, puzzled. She stepped forward: her voice was composed. 'That still doesn't explain why he would pull you in. Not if you've no idea—'

'I'd set a watch on her flat,' Eric explained wearily. 'The man watching got beaten up. And Cindy was then virtually beaten to death. Bateman seems to think if I hadn't interfered, it wouldn't have happened. He seems to believe it might have been done by this man Reilly, and he's convinced I'm tied into it, in some way, through Scarn.'

'The watch on the flat,' Dorothy Farnon said tightly. 'Why—'

'She used to be Svensson's girl-friend. I went to see her. There was someone waiting in the street when I came out. I had a feeling it could have been Svensson. So I asked Jackie Parton, anyway, the girl's dead, and somehow I've got into something I don't understand.'

'And you feel responsible,' Dorothy Farnon said quietly.

'That's it.' Eric put his head back on the chair and half closed his eyes. He was tired, weary with the dull ache behind his eyes, the unexpected, sharp needles of pain that came intermittently. 'Yes, somehow I've blundered into something and it's all pointless, particularly since Bateman insists that I must have been watching Cindy Jackson for other reasons. He doesn't believe me, because he has proof that Svensson is dead.'

He closed his eyes and the room was silent. But there was something strained about the silence and after a few seconds the tension was communicated to him. He opened his eyes. Dorothy Farnon was staring at Dick Kenton, her mouth set, her fingers crooked at her side. Kenton himself was sitting hunched forward, his grimy fingers cradling the can of beer. He was glaring at Eric, struggling with the words that were locked in his chest. There was something in his eyes too, an expression Eric had seen before but could not completely read, beyond the signs of strain and panic and latent fear. 'What's the matter?' he asked.

The words came out reluctantly, mumbling, almost incoherent. 'Bateman . . . the coppers . . . they're wrong. That proof is rubbish. There's something funny going on . . . I can't make it out—'

'What are you trying to say?' Eric asked sharply.

'Svensson's alive.'

'But you can't –'

'Svensson is alive! *I've seen him!* Whatever Bateman says, he's lying! Svensson came back to Tyneside about two weeks ago. Give me twenty-four hours and I'll prove it!'

CHAPTER 5

From the windows of the flat in Gosforth the lights on the Durham hills were visible as a twinkling chain, gleaming and coruscating in the soft northern darkness. Anne had always loved the night: the popular image of the North was of cold winds and empty beaches; people rarely spoke of the way the night sky appeared, pale blue at the horizon, deep, dark blue above, but always a summer colour, not black, not suffocating, but a soft, gentle hue, the kind you could walk under and see under and make love under. It was one of the reasons why, in choosing a flat for business purposes in Newcastle, to avoid late evening drives back to Sedleigh Hall, she had insisted upon a top-floor address. It still gave her the feeling of freedom, and she could still enjoy the open Northumberland skies. Now, with Eric.

She had been unable to hide her anxiety when he had phoned, to tell her he did not feel up to making his way back to the Hall. She had immediately agreed to see him at the flat, and when she arrived he was already asleep in the chair near the window. She had made no attempt to wake him; instead, she sat down quietly, facing him, watching his face, listening to his breathing.

She remembered how tall he had looked when first they had met; he was a big man, but lean, and soft-moving. She had liked his face: his eyes were gentle, and capable of understanding, and his mouth was generous, though she had seen it hard and stubborn. He *could* be a stubborn man, and not least in his refusal to give way under the shock of glaucoma, the destruction of one career, and now surgery. It would all have been so much easier if only he was the kind of man who could accept what she had to offer: love, security, and a degree of wealth. Yet perhaps if he had been the kind of man who could accept that, she would have loved him less. There lay the irony of their situation. The obstacles he raised were important to him, though not to her, but though she denied it vehemently, she would have thought less of him as a man, had he not held such scruples. He was wrong, but she loved him for it.

Even so, this business was different. He should not have entered employment so soon; the anxiety was etched on his face, lines around his mouth, and for the first time she was becoming aware of the fact he was twenty years older than she. Eric Ward was a man of strong constitution, but surgery and tension were running him down. She was determined it should stop.

When he woke, he was obviously pleased to see her. She quite deliberately made no fuss, but gave him a glass of wine — one would do no harm — and then busied herself in the kitchen, making a lasagne for them both. Only when they both took coffee afterwards did she ask him what had happened.

'Is it that obvious?' he asked wearily.

'You look ill, Eric. Yes, it's that obvious.'

And he told her — about the girl called Cindy Jackson, about Detective-Superintendent Bateman, and, finally, about the man called Svensson. As he spoke she said nothing, but a cold chill moved slowly through her, icing her bones, touching her flesh and making it crawl. She had control of her features, and she kept her fingers stiffly wound together, hands gripped tightly, but the erratic movement inside her breast, the thunder of her heart, seemed loud enough and obvious enough to make it clear she was badly scared.

She finished her coffee before she spoke. 'Eric, you seem to think that the key to the whole matter lies with Philip Scarn.'

'Jackie Parton thinks so,' he corrected her.

'But you also said Bateman—'

'That's right. He's tying in Scarn with the killing, and Reilly, and all the rest of it. But there's something still not quite right. Something odd in the whole business. Why does Bateman insist that Svensson is dead — in face of the phone calls, my own sighting of the man, and now Kenton's telling me he can bring me proof within twenty-four hours? I tell you, Anne, I feel so helpless.' He laughed shortly, contemptuously. 'In a way I feel it's all tied up with this damned glaucoma. When I last saw the surgeon, you'll remember he wasn't very encouraging. The likelihood, he said, was that I'd suffer from limited vision. A limited vision. That's how I feel about this whole thing. It's as though I'm staring down a telescope, seeking the truth, but I can't see beyond the area scanned by the tunnel of light. I can't see the fringes, make out the motives, determine the links. If they even exist at all! A limited vision. Hell's flames—'

She recognized his sudden desperation and cut across it. 'Darling the first thing you must do is get out of the Scarn thing. If Bateman says—'

'*Bateman!*' There was thinly veiled anger shading into contempt in his voice. He got up, walked across to the window and stood staring out to the lights on the distant moorland above Consett. 'Bateman was quick to tell me Svensson was dead. He regretted letting slip the name Paddy Reilly. He wanted *me* to tell him about Scarn's involvement with Cindy Jackson. But I don't like bloody Detective-Superintendent Bateman.'

'But as a senior officer—'

'Don't say it, Anne.' He shook his head regretfully. 'The stink of police corruption can rise high. You won't remember ex-Chief Constable Starling. He rose swiftly, and he ended up with a nice piece of land in Northumberland, riding to the Hunt, the full, respected social scene. But there were examples, cases where he deliberately fixed evidence to get convictions, clearly instructed serving officers to behave . . . ah, the hell with it!'

'You'll have to back out of this contract with Philip Scarn,' Anne said quietly. 'You'll have to do it, Eric: the whole thing is ripping you apart.'

'I've got to see him first,' Eric said, 'I've got to get to the bottom of this whole thing.'

And something died inside her at the words.

* * *

The girl in the white shirtwaist and grey skirt explained to him that Mr Scarn was in conference at that time and would be involved for most of the morning. She would see to it that he was informed Mr Ward required an urgent appointment. Would Mr Ward be in his own office during the course of the afternoon?

Mr Ward would.

There were files there for him to go through, though he did it half-heartedly. Anne was right: he could no longer work for Philip Scarn, whatever the realities of the man's involvement with the death of Cindy Jackson. The tension, the uncertainty, the anxiety, it was all looming too large. The atropine he was using had its effect, but according to the surgeon it should not have been strictly necessary, at least in the dosage Eric was now using. The man had insisted Eric took things easy, had doubted in his tone the wisdom of Eric's taking a job. Now, Eric wondered why the hell he had acted so quickly at all. Stubbornness, pride, independence: they could yet be the death of him, he thought grimly as he went through the files.

There was nothing among the papers that gave him any further information, any clue that might lead him to a reappraisal of the whole situation. Detective-Superintendent Bateman had started to say something but cut himself off, exploded into anger at Eric Ward. Now, it seemed, only Philip Scarn would be able to clear things up to Eric's satisfaction.

The chance did not come until three o'clock that afternoon.

Philip Scarn breezed into the office carelessly, smiling, white teeth flashing against the tan of his features, white handkerchief spilling from the breast pocket of his dark blue suit. His shirt was pale blue silk, patterned, elegant; his bearing was confident, his mood elated. He came in, walked up to Eric and clapped a hand on his shoulder, grinning. 'Well, Eric, that's a good deal settled: you'll be able to get to work at Sunderland straight away. Didn't need your contacts on this one at all, as it happened: the recession in the area means some property developers have had their fingers burned these last few years, and now I've snapped up a plum site, just where I want in. Come Monday, I'll want contracts prepared, because I need to move fast on this one, but that shouldn't be a problem for you, hey? Things are beginning to look good, Eric!' He sat down in the chair in front of Eric's desk, and looked up to him where he was still standing. 'Now then, you wanted to see me. Problems?'

'You could put it like that.'

'Well, fire away.' Scarn waved magnanimously.

Eric Ward sat down and held the other man's glance. 'I'd like you to explain to me what part you had to play in Cindy Jackson's death.'

Something faded in Philip Scarn's smile: he held it, but the edges of his mouth were suddenly hard, and there was no longer any pleasure in his eyes. 'What was that again?' he asked.

'Cindy Jackson.'

'I've never heard of her.' Philip Scarn fumbled in the pocket of his jacket, extracted a cigarette while Eric watched silently. He lit the cigarette with a gold lighter, blew smoke into the air contentedly and then grimaced at Eric through the smoke. 'Now just what are you on about?'

'I was hauled into police headquarters yesterday. I was questioned about the girl's death. The suggestion was made that I was in some degree responsible. That suggestion was linked to your name.'

'You don't say!' Philip Scarn inclined his head to one side in doubt. 'Who was it saw you?'

'Detective-Superintendent Bateman.'

'Is that right? And he mentioned my name?'

Eric stared stonily at his employer. 'I have the feeling you're playing for time, Mr Scarn. Time to think.'

Philip Scarn nodded, his eyes avoiding Eric's. He fiddled with the cuff of his shirt, then nodded again. 'So what else did Bateman say to you? Any other names?'

'Yes. Reilly. Paddy Reilly.'

The smile came back on Scarn's face, slithering unpleasantly across his features. His eyes gleamed. 'So Reilly is involved. Interesting.'

'You know something about all this, Scarn. *I* want to know. I've been accused—'

'Because you're working for me?' Scarn challenged.

'It would seem so.'

'Bit far-fetched, isn't it? I mean, I've never heard of this girl, and—'

'I know about Johnston O'Connor, too.'

For one brief moment a glint of alarm appeared in Scarn's eyes but it was quickly damped and the smile slithered back, under control again. 'Just *what* do you know about Johnston O'Connor?'

Eric took a deep breath. 'I know that the *entertainment* industry in the North-East is under the control of O'Connor. I know that the red light areas and the night-clubs, and probably the gambling clubs also, are linked to him, so that he would certainly resent the kind of intrusion you're planning in your business ventures. And I think you were fully aware of his existence and of the problems that might arise if you were to establish some sort of competition in the area, affecting his interests.'

Scarn grimaced, shrugged diffidently. 'So . . . ?'

'One of O'Connor's henchmen is called Reilly: Paddy Reilly. He's responsible for the prostitution ring O'Connor runs. And Detective-Superintendent Bateman feels he's linked in some way to you.'

'I can't be responsible for the worms that crawl in Bateman's head,' Scarn said coolly. 'But go on.'

'Reilly is a good-looking man—'

'A handsome bastard, I know,' Scarn admitted, with a faint unpleasant smile.

'And at the beginning, at least, he recruited girls himself. One of them may have been Cindy Jackson. I'd set a watch on her, and then she got beaten. She died as a result of the beating.'

'I tell you, I never heard of Cindy Jackson.' Even as he said it a slight shadow touched Scarn's eyes, the flicker of a memory, dark, momentarily uncontrolled, but quickly hidden. 'So what's this got to do with me?

'Bateman thinks—'

Bateman!'

'Bateman thinks Reilly is responsible for the beating: at least that's what I guess. And you're involved, because Bateman assumed I'd set the watch on the girl because of my involvement with you.'

'But you can't have done.'

Eric nodded grimly. 'I had my own reasons. But I still want to know where you fit in.'

Scarn inspected the glowing end of his cigarette with an affected concern. His mouth twisted unpleasantly. 'Mr Ward, you and Bateman have something in common as far as I'm concerned. His, and your, desires are a matter of complete indifference to me.'

'Scarn—'

Eric stopped as Philip Scarn raised a hand imperiously. 'I will pay you this compliment, however, Ward. You are great on ethics, is that right? You believe in, for instance, the trust relationship that is established between solicitor and client. If I want advice from you, and need to give you certain facts, the statements I make are — how do you describe it in legal terms? — privileged?'

'That's right,' Eric replied tightly. 'I wouldn't be able to disclose such facts without your express approval.'

'Fine. I thought that's the way it would be. All right, I'll come clean with you, Ward, and then maybe you can tell *me* where Bateman would seem to think I tie in with Cindy Jackson.' He drew thoughtfully on his cigarette and then, with an expression of distaste, stubbed it out. 'The whole things goes back a few years now, since the time when I first set up in business in the North-East. You'll remember the development boom in the sixties?'

'I remember.'

'I was in on it. Some judicious purchases of land on the northern outskirts of the city, a few good building contracts, and I was launched. I was well on my way to my first million — and I have your assurance that this conversation is covered by privilege, Ward?'

'You have.'

'Well, I quickly became aware that in order to really make money in such a boom, you had to be prepared to *spend* money, too. There were palms to be greased: committees had members with power, who liked to feel they were, shall we say, *appreciated*, when they came to decisions favourable to a particular contractor.'

'You're talking about bribery of councillors,' Eric said grimly, 'and officials.'

'Precisely. And it worked, believe me, it worked. But I was careful. Others weren't, and got prison sentences as a result of it. Me, well, two things happened. In the first instance, I decided to keep a steady, low profile: I moved into industrial unit building, and I never got *personally* involved in the corruption side. It's surprising how many so-called professional people will be prepared to front for you, in such a situation. For their own continued professional fees, of course.'

Eric knew what he meant. Accountants, architects, lawyers too, they all held among their ranks men and women who were prepared to turn a blind eye to corruption, for their own professional advantage. He had known some, and not all of them had received prison sentences. He eyed Scarn carefully. 'You think maybe I would fit into that kind of category.'

A contemptuous smile appeared on Scarn's face. He shrugged. 'I meant what I said to you in London. I wanted your experience, expertise and contacts. But, I will admit I considered that when maybe the going got a bit rough, you'd be a man prepared to . . . *bend* a bit? After all, there would be few other prospects open to you, with your record, and your . . . disability.'

There was a tight, angry feeling in Eric Ward's chest. He held back the words that he wanted to say; instead, he said, in a calm tone, 'All right. So what happened then?'

Scarn shook his head. 'Things began to change subtly. I had the ends all tied up, it seemed: politicians, a couple of county hall men, professional accountants, an architect . . . it was all pretty sweet. And then I lost a couple of good deals. I was surprised, but not too unhappy. After all, it made things look a bit more legitimate, If you know what I mean, me losing a few deals. Unfortunately, It kept happening.'

'You didn't have it tied up as tightly as you'd thought?'

'Oh, I had it tied up all right,' Scarn said softly. 'But the fact was, someone else moved in. And I still don't know how.'

'Another property developer?'

'You remember James Christie?'

Eric nodded. The man had flared on the north-eastern business scene like an explosive rocket, but had died as quickly, convicted of corrupt practices and jailed for two years. 'He was your rival?'

'I thought so. But he happened too fast, and blew up too quickly. There was someone else behind him, smoothing his path — and in the end ensuring that Christie took the full weight of the blow personally.'

'Who?'

'Johnston O'Connor.'

Eric stared at Scarn in surprise. Slowly he shook his head. 'I don't understand. As far as I understand it, O'Connor has been concerned only with the shady side of the entertainment business. You're telling me he was also mixed up in the construction field?'

Scarn scratched his cheek thoughtfully. 'Not in a big way. He simply made contacts for Christie and took a rake-off from the profits. He set up a few local politicians; and he acquired one or two prime sites for his own interests, gambling premises, mainly. But in doing so—'

'He hurt you,' Eric said, beginning to understand at last.

'That's right.' Scarn's tone was soft but there was no hiding the bitterness in his voice. 'He supported Christie for as long as the man was viable, then he left him to face prosecution. In so doing, he cut me out — and worse. Somehow, *somehow* he destroyed two important bids for me, bids that would have made me a millionaire. The Cenden complex, and the Framegate Shopping Centre: they went to Christie, who blew the whole deals with his stupid bribery. And his bids undercut mine — *because he knew what mine were*. I never could find precisely how it was done, things moved too fast. I saw what was happening and got out of Tyneside, built up my business in the south. But the whispers I *have* had were that Reilly fixed it, Reilly was the man who got his hands on my bids, and now you tell me . . . this girl, Cindy Jackson . . .' He paused, lost in thought, dredging back over the years, seeking faces, names, facts. 'There was a girl in my contracts department, a clerk . . . Cynthia . . . Cynthia Something . . . I wonder . . .'

'Your return to the North,' Eric cut in, angry, but still in control. 'It was never going to be a straight business situation.'

Scarn stared at him, his pale eyes hard. 'I'm a rich man, Mr Ward, but a dissatisfied one. I can *afford* to come back north now. And I can afford my revenge. Johnston O'Connor backed Christie and effectively drove me out. That's rankled a long time. You're absolutely right. I've come back to do to O'Connor what he did to me: with interest. I'm going to break his business.'

'And it's no secret.'

Scarn smiled wolfishly. 'I never intended it to be. You see, Ward, if you make your intentions plain, people *react*. They get flurried, they get anxious, they make assumptions about your plans — even if you don't really have any, at least not specifically. And the reactions are often ill-calculated. People *expose* themselves in such circumstances, and I'm wondering now whether Reilly — and behind him, O'Connor — has now exposed himself foolishly. After all, the *police* have been interested ever since they heard I was coming north; my intentions were something they could latch on to with interest — and it would seem they too believe Cindy Jackson was somehow involved. It's why they'll have been annoyed by your interference. You, of course, were the unknown factor, but it seems you've been useful, stirring up the hornets' nest.'

Eric Ward thought of the battered girl lying on the floor of the flat in Byker and said angrily, 'I don't like your methods, Mr Scarn.'

'You don't have to. Just follow my orders.'

'I don't know that I can do that any more.'

Scarn stared at him coldly. There was no longer any veneer of politeness: whatever impression Scarn gave to his business contemporaries there was no doubt that underneath it all was a hard, vicious, vengeful man. 'You've had a troubled life of recent years, Mr Ward. I could make it more so.'

'I don't disbelieve it.'

'On the other hand, you've nothing to hurt me with. What I've said . . . privileged communications . . . if I read you right, Ward, you can't talk about what I've said.'

'I—'

'Beside, you're probably acting hastily, aren't you? When you've had time to think things over, this foolish suggestion that you wish to leave my employ will be set against your general background, and you'll change your mind. After all, what else is there for you at the moment? Where else would you get such a retainer? Think it over, my friend, think it over carefully. And either way, remember: I'm a man who bears grudges, and you'd be no exception if you give me cause.'

The barely veiled threat was not lost upon Eric and he thought about it as he sat in his office during the rest of the afternoon. He could now understand why the police had been so interested in his involvement with Scarn; why Jackie Parton had been so nervous about asking questions regarding O'Connor; and why there had been a general reluctance on the part of magistrates and others to discuss seriously with him the matter of licences for Scarn's operations in the North-East. They had all been aware of the problems that could arise: they had all been waiting, in a sense, just as Philip Scarn himself had been waiting, for someone to make a wrong move. And now it seemed as though Johnston O'Connor and his henchman Reilly had perhaps made that wrong move.

It was a thought that came to him again when he left the office at five and stepped out into the street. There was a tall, young, muscular but polite man in a business suit at the kerb. He stepped towards Eric.

'I wonder whether you'd mind accompanying me for a short drive? My employer would like to meet you.'

'Your employer?'

'Mr Johnston O'Connor.'

* * *

The hotel room had an air of expensive vulgarity about it that was heightened by the angular, elaborate furniture, the Chinese rugs, the sharp glittering pieces of abstract sculpture. It contained a board table and was used for business meetings; its thick curtains and double doors ensured privacy at a price.

The man seated near the window could clearly afford that price.

He wore a steel-grey suit of an elegant cut, with a shapely folded handkerchief in the breast pocket. His shirt was a light blue and open-necked and he held in his hand a cut-glass tumbler that contained whisky. His fingers were long and slim, curling lightly around the glass. He watched Eric Ward as he was ushered forward and then Ward's escort was dismissed with a nod.

'I thought it was time we met, Mr Ward.'

His voice was careful yet edged with ice and Eric made no reply, contenting himself with studying the man's face. O'Connor was perhaps in his mid-fifties, with thinning, dark, carefully brushed hair and heavy, severe eyebrows. His skin was pale, his features lean, and his eyes were of the kind behind which controlled anger seemed constantly to boil. That he was accustomed to command was obvious; that he was dangerous was something Eric had already gathered from his conversations with Jackie Parton, Bateman, and, earlier today, Philip Scarn.

'I thought it was time we met,' O'Connor repeated, 'because I like to have a close look at men who might find themselves in . . . opposition to me.'

'I don't know what you mean,' Eric said woodenly. He had come to see O'Connor because he was curious, but he was as yet determined to keep the curiosity hidden.

'Oh, come now, you work for Philip Scarn, don't you?' O'Connor smiled thinly, wickedly. 'For the time being, at least.'

'What's that supposed to mean?'

'Merely that you've backed a losing horse. You'll never clear the legal ground for Scarn. I'll kill every option he tries to take up, and I'll make sure the bastard goes back south with his tail between his legs like a whipped dog. Your job isn't going to last long, Mr Ward and my advice is to get out while you can still salvage some professional reputation from the involvement.'

'And how do you propose to block the planning applications Scarn has filed?'

'I know a lot of people. They know what side their bread is buttered. So should you.' O'Connor paused, eyeing Eric coldly. 'You've caused me a bit of bother, my friend, and I don't like that. It's time it stopped.'

'I don't know what you're talking about.'

'I think you do.'

Eric was silent for several seconds, thinking, and then he nodded. 'All right, perhaps I do . . . now. In a sense this . . . summons confirms it. Philip Scarn has an old score to settle with you and he's out to give you some tough competition in the "entertainment" field. But my involvement has been quite minimal, believe me.'

'I wouldn't have said so — particularly so far as one unfortunate incident was concerned.'

'You mean Cindy Jackson's murder?'

'Did I mention a name?'

'The police think your man, Reilly, killed her — maybe not intending to — and that it's connected with Scarn.'

The cold eyes shifted, anger starting to simmer behind them more clearly now. 'If there *was* a connection with Scarn, how did you get to know about it, Mr Ward?'

'*I didn't* know about it.'

'I don't believe you.'

'I don't give a damn whether you do or not.'

The silence grew around them. O'Connor fingered his glass, controlling his temper which was growing by the moment. 'You set a watch on her flat; Scarn must have been on to her. You'd have been trying to screw some information out of her.'

'Information? Such as the fact that she passed company secrets to Paddy Reilly, and then to you, years ago? Secrets about building bids, secrets that helped you tumble Scarn down south, and leave yourself free to run Tyneside the way you want to? You're a bloody fool, O'Connor. Scarn never knew that. I went to see that girl, put a watch on her for an entirely different reason, unconnected with Scarn, a private reason! If you killed her, or had her killed, it was the stupid mistake Scarn and the police have been waiting for!'

'Her death was nothing to do with me. I never ordered—'

'The fact is she *is* dead, the police think your man Reilly is responsible, and if I think they're barking up the wrong tree, I certainly don't mind if they can put you where you belong, even on a trumped-up charge!'

O'Connor eyed him coldly for a moment. 'So you believe me when I said I didn't order that girl's killing.'

'I just have my own views about it.'

'Either way, you're Scarn's man, and you've been bothering me so I felt it was time for an unfriendly warning.'

Eric Ward was suddenly incensed. He had already received one warning today, from Philip Scarn, and his own sense of involvement in Cindy Jackson's death was acute, whatever he might say. He leaned forward, glaring at O'Connor. 'Listen, I don't give a damn what you and Scarn get up to. You can cut each other's throats for all I care. You run shady operations up here, and Scarn wants to muscle in. It's nothing to do with me. But I'll take no warning from either of you. As far as I'm concerned, you can both go to hell!'

'And as far as I'm concerned, Ward, I've had enough of you! I'm not accustomed to being called a fool, and stupid, and I don't like having my toes trodden on by half-blind dimwit lawyers like you.' O'Connor stood up suddenly, and some of the whisky in his glass spilled on to his shirt. He ignored it as, with his voice trembling with suppressed rage he said, 'Stay out of my business, stay away from my people. If you don't, I'll make damn sure you stay out of it all — *permanently!*'

* * *

There was nothing more to be said after that; O'Connor had pressed a bell-push and the polite, muscular young man had entered to take Eric back to the car.

The interview left Eric angry, dissatisfied, and still with the feeling there was something missing in the whole equation. Svensson. The police insisted he was dead, and that Cindy Jackson's death was tied in with a Scarn O'Connor battle. But there was another explanation: Svensson, back on Tyneside, finding his girl-friend involved with the O'Connor organization and seeking revenge. It could have been enough to make him attack her in a blind rage.

It was certainly a theory preferable to Bateman's, which suggested the girl had died in Byker because Eric Ward had set a watch on her. Yet it was not a theory he could put to the test until Dick Kenton did as he had promised.

The chance did not come until late the next afternoon. He was clearing his desk when the call came through on the switchboard. The caller was ex-Detective-Inspector Dick Kenton, breathless, and excited.

'That you, Eric?'

'Yes.'

'You wanted proof; you wanted Svensson; I've set it up. Can you meet me this evening?'

'When?'

'Eight o'clock.'

'Where?'

There was a brief hesitation, as though Dick Kenton was weighing up possibilities. 'You know the Prudhoe Street Mission?'

'Top of Westgate Hill? I know it.'

'Meet me there.'

Eric hesitated. It would be necessary to contact Anne, to tell her he'd be late. She could worry unnecessarily, otherwise. He was suddenly aware that his hand gripping the telephone receiver was damp with nervous tension, at the thought of his meeting Svensson. It was nevertheless what he had been wanting. 'All right,' he said to Kenton, his mouth dry and his tone brusque. 'I'll be there at eight o'clock, sharp.'

When he tried to ring Anne the switchboard was unresponsive: the girl had gone home, and the phone was dead.

* * *

The central railway station in Newcastle had received a facelift: the grand, solid structure erected in the 1850s and eroded over the years had been stripped, taken down, and re-erected until the scene surrounding the station was closer now to the original than it had been for a hundred years, if one discounted the traffic, and the new office blocks behind the statue of Robert Stephenson, and the one-way system bypassing the West Road.

Eric took an early evening meal in the Viking Restaurant and they walked past the city wall northwards, heading for the rise of Westgate Hill. The night-clubs were not yet open: the cinemas still lethargic, and the early evening traffic running into the city not yet heavy as he walked slowly up the rise, past the Assembly Rooms, towards Arthur's Hill with its towering, soulless blocks of flats overlooking the narrow terraced streets that sliced their way down towards Scotswood. Westgate Hill had changed since the days, years ago, when he had patrolled there as a raw constable: the cinemas had closed, motorcycle shops had opened, small businesses had put up shutters against the recession and open spaces were levelling out towards the river, heralding new visions regarding the west end of the city, visions that would yet have to fight the traditions of the past. Just below the brow of the hill the Seconds Shop still flourished, the Mecca for early morning West End inhabitants, where they could buy yesterday's bread at reduced rates, a place out of time, a memory of the depressed 'thirties, yet flourishing after fifty years of affluence. The Prudhoe Street Mission had not changed, either.

It was solid, unmoving, seemingly immutable. It stood on the crossroads at the top of Westgate Hill, as proud of its present existence as of its past benefactions, unmoved by the loss of the big lamp that had acted as a beacon and a landmark for generations of West Enders, and as sturdily declaring the time with its clock-tower now as it had done since its Victorian erection. It brooded over the traffic that surged past its base, but it had seen masts on the river, and football-fanatical hordes flowing into St James's Park, and the destruction of slums, the erection of new hovels. There was nothing new under the Mission sun: all had been observed before, and it waited straddling the hill brow, for eternity to touch and translate it, perhaps into rubble. But not yet.

It was an odd place for Dick Kenton to choose to meet Eric Ward.

And yet perhaps not so odd. Svensson had returned to Tyneside, and would have been seeking old haunts. The sprawl of Walker and Byker and Wallsend to the east had changed for him as an environment: so had the west end of the town with the opening out of the terraced areas with bulldozers, the creation of new spaces. But something of the old days still pulsed in the West End: it held a defiance that suggested it would never lose its sense of place in the history of the city. And it would still hold attractions, contacts, involvements for a man who knew the river, and slipped back to old moorings, old occupations, and familiar opportunities. The roar could still drift up when Newcastle United scored; the surprisingly affluent cars could still park in dingy side streets; the old myths could still be trotted out, regurgitated in West End pubs; and the refurbished houses and new terraces fooled no one with their bright brown brick.

But Dick Kenton was late.

Eric stood just below the corner, away from the entrance to the Mission's three-road frontage and watched, and waited, but there was no sign of Kenton. Several times cars had crawled up from Elswick and hesitated uncertainly at the lights; on three occasions men had walked around the corner in the fading light and looked as though they wanted to talk to someone, perhaps anyone. But the light began to die, the street lamps were glowing orange in the city below, Eric Ward was still waiting, and Dick Kenton had not kept his rendezvous.

The urchin came as a surprise.

He was perhaps nine years old. In a different generation he would have worn ragged short trousers, but now it was

131

stained, torn, ragged jeans. His predecessors would perhaps have been shoeless, but he was shod in scuffed, broken baseball shoes. For the rest, he ran true to form. His hair was spiky and long, his face dirty, his eyes knowledgeable, old, curious and wary. The elbows of his woollen jumper, probably purchased from a second-hand shop where at least three languages, far east of Geordie, were spoken, were worn and ragged, and one of his front teeth was missing, another blackened. He knew where he was; there was nothing behind him and nothing ahead of him, except that which he grabbed, caught, squeezed for himself.

'Mister?'

'Yes?'

'You lookin' for someone?'

The boy's eyes were large, brown and restless. He was lightly balanced on the balls of his feet: Eric had seen so many young lads in the old days, poised to run.

'What's it to you, son?' he asked quietly, watching the boy carefully.

'I got a message.'

'For . . . ?'

'Somebody called Ward.'

The use of the surname was challenging, a refusal to accept that adults had any claim to superiority in his nine-year-old world. His father, if he had one, thought Ward, would be a hard man.

'I'm called Eric Ward.'

'You expectin' someone?'

'That's right.'

'Wassis name, then?'

Eric smiled faintly: it was curious how, even in someone so young and hardened, there could still be a sense of duty that overlaid his cynicism. The boy had been paid to deliver a message: he would keep his bargain.

'I was expecting to meet a man called Kenton.'

'He can't make it,' the boy announced abruptly, and thrust out his hand. 'Told me to give yer this.'

The note in his hand was grubby and soiled; Eric took the wrist rather than the note and there was a sudden jerking tension which as suddenly relaxed. The boy watched coldly as Eric uncurled the fingers, extracted the note, and retained his grip on the slim, wiry wrist.

He read it, as the boy stood passively beside him and the evening traffic spun down the hill to the city. It was brief, handwritten, and to the point.

Shurrock's Drift. Within the hour. And for God's sake, alone. D. K.

Eric opened his mouth to ask the boy to describe Dick Kenton but the moment was seized: a sudden, swift twist of the wrist and his grip was broken, the boy dancing away out of reach, mocking, triumphant, screeching defiance. 'Canny bastard, think you are, don't yer? You with them glasses, get knotted, mister!'

Eric raised his hand, trying to stop the boy, poised as he was to flee across the road and into the streets of Scotswood. 'Wait! The man who gave you this—'

'Me mam told me not to speak to strangers!' the boy yelled in delight, and scuttered across the road, causing a red sports car to blare, and swerve at the green lights. 'You can sod off, mister! Done me job.' The remainder of the obscenities were lost to Eric as the boy ran down into Elswick Road and was swallowed up in the awakening traffic filtering up from Rye Hill, with its grand new college buildings and a population that could remember grimier times.'

He looked again at the note. He did not know Dick Kenton's handwriting, but the initials were there, and it had been delivered by someone expecting a meeting between Kenton and Eric Ward. Nevertheless, something crawled in Eric Ward's stomach, the memory of old misgivings, and he stood at the entrance to the Prudhoe Street Mission with its garish shop fronts and he stared at the note and he was uncertain.

Yet he knew, in a sense, that he had no choice; had never had any choice. Slowly, he turned and walked back down the hill towards the Central Station where he would be certain of getting a taxi.

He directed the driver to take the road west, and then north.

* * *

Eric Ward was as aware as anyone of the contrasts that could be demonstrated by the Northumberland and Durham countryside. South of the river, the scar of Consett was set in breath-taking countryside to which the iron-red skies of yesterday had added an industrially-enhanced effect, now ended for ever. To the north, once the orange glow of Newcastle began to fade and the mist-hung banks of the Tyne were lost under the ridges of the river valley, the countryside opened out into long, swinging ranges, hills folding upon one another, the promise of distant beckoning heights in the Cheviots, the surprises of sudden, hidden tarns nestling among thick clumps of trees, tiny stone bridges straddling sparkling streams, complacent farms protected from the January winds that could come sweeping down, snow-laden from the Scottish moorlands. But every hill climbed gave a view of distant chimneys at Blyth, and a turn in the road could expose a greening, opencast scar. There had been ancient whisky stills in this countryside in the eighteenth century, remote and safe from Revenue men, but while they had disappeared the debris of later activity had not: cast-down pit shafts, boiler houses rust red beside the rivers, disused winding wheels stark against the pale blue evening sky.

Shurrock's Drift lay at the head of a small glen, sheltered from east winds by a shoulder of gorse-laden hillside and a summer solitude for lovers who could escape the throngs of the city by way of a twenty-minute drive. The glen itself was crowded with wild flowers that had softened the straight lines of disused track, once used to trundle coal down to the roadway and, eventually, the staiths on the Tyne; the mine itself was a deserted spot, not frequented by Newcastle visitors since the glen branched to the left, more pleasingly and secretively, with overhanging trees, a brook that tumbled erratically down gentle slopes, and pine-needled spaces designed for soft words. Eric Ward paid off the taxi-driver at the entrance to the glen; returning would not be difficult if Kenton did not keep the rendezvous, since a village lay just a mile distant. And the note had stressed Eric should come alone.

Within minutes he had left the worn track frequented by those who normally came to the glen, and was walking along the old railway line towards the drift itself. The track was wide enough for a car, and as far as he could observe there had been some traffic along this way recently: the thought struck him, coldly, that it might have been Svensson. Then the roadway rose, thrusting under alder and silver birch overhanging the track, before it dipped gently into the basin that was Shurrock's Drift.

The evidence of its old activity was still there in profusion. The track widened, opened into a long circular area where trams had been turned, filled from the overhead dumpers; the iron circle was still there in the centre, rust red and unused for thirty years or more. Beyond the ruined loaders, clustered at the edge of the area, were the dilapidated remains of the wheelhouse and the mine office. The walls gaped open to the sky, the windows black interstices against the grey, solid stone. Eric stood there and stared about him. There was no sign of anyone else in the glen or at the mine itself, and as the evening darkened about him a soft, cold wind began to rise, rustling the long grass that had grown over the broken tracks that led to the pit opening.

Eric stared at the drift itself. The semi-circular entry, a black scar in the green of the hillside, had been fenced off many years ago, but the iron railings were broken and twisted, vandalized so that entry to the drift was easy for child, or man. From where he stood he could hear the slow drip of water, and the tiny stream that emerged from the drift, the collection of moisture percolating through the arch of the tunnel, seemed to glisten blackly in the faint light.

The breeze was cool on his cheek, and he was suddenly aware of the tremor of his hand, the prelude to the old prickling that would soon begin at the back of his eyes: It was the tension getting to him, the uncertainty that was gathering as he waited and saw no sign of the man he expected. Kenton's note had held a ring of urgency, and he had insisted that Eric meet him within the hour but as the darkness grew about him, and the prickling behind his eyes increased, bringing the first needle points of pain that would cause the uncontrollable shuddering he knew so well, Eric knew that he would not be able to wait. If Kenton did not arrive within minutes, Eric would have to leave, walk along the roadway to the village and phone for a taxi from the pub there. He stood uncertainly, staring at the entrance to Shurrock's Drift, and then he turned, looked across towards the shadowed stone of the old wheelhouse.

A stab of pain, almost delicious in its intensity, lanced across the nerve ends behind his eyes and he raised a hand, rubbed gently at his eyes, but it was an almost dismissive gesture, for a slow coldness was beginning to creep through his body. The boy had fled before he could be questioned about Kenton; Eric Ward had not seen Kenton's handwriting in years and certainly had no idea what it looked like; there was only the boy's knowledge that Kenton was due to meet Ward at the Prudhoe Street Mission to offer proof that the note had been genuine.

But it was not impossible that someone else could have learned of the meeting; someone who would wish to draw Eric Ward away from the city, to a deserted spot like Shurrock's Drift. Not impossible, and easy to achieve: just give a young lad on the street a brief, uncommunicative note.

The walls of the wheelhouse had collapsed at one side but at the other they stood solidly, shadowing the small yard at the back, with its narrow entry beside the old mine office. Unsteadily, Eric began to walk towards the wheelhouse. His hand was shaking again, but he was hardly aware of the pain that was scratching at him: he was certain now that the man he had been looking for, the man who had made the threatening calls, the man whom Detective-Superintendent Bateman insisted was dead, was here, at Shurrock's Drift, waiting, watching in the darkness.

'*Svensson?*'

Eric's voice echoed in the clearing, skittering a parody of the word among the littered wheelhouse, dying against the soft rise of the hillside beyond. The man was here, Eric knew it with a terrible, angry certainty, and the anger pumped blood to his head, drove away the onset of the cat claws behind his eyes, pushed him forward towards the wheelhouse.

'*Svensson!*' He called the name again, and walked quickly over the littered ground, stumbling slightly as he came to the entry at the side of the wheelhouse. And there, half hidden in the yard he saw it, the metallic shine of a car, pulled deep into the yard, crouching against the broken wall at the back where it was twisted with alder, springing almost from the stone itself. Angrily, Eric strode forward into the entry, opened his mouth to call Svensson's name once again, draw him from his hiding place, but the word never came. He was briefly aware that anger had caused him to lose caution; there was a flurry of dark movement to his right, a burly figure emerging from behind the broken wall, and then the blow took him at the nape of the neck. He stumbled, fell forward to his knees and tried to rise again, hand outstretched, attempting to ward off the second blow that was sure to come.

But there was only a flash of light and the cold of the stone entry against his face, and then there was the darkness.

* * *

Later, much later, when his senses took in his surroundings and he fought against the muzziness and the pain and the throbbing in his head and his hands, it was the persistent dripping sound that told him where he was. The blackness about him was complete and he realized there was no sky above him; the cold was clammy and pervasive, seeming to eat into his bones. He was on his knees, half-lying against a wet stone wall and the regular dripping sound came from the water percolating through the roof. Gradually, he became aware of the rag material that had been stuffed into his mouth and the roughly improvised gag that held it in place, to prevent his calling out for help. He tried to move but there was something above him — a heavy baulk of timber, and his hands were close to it, firmly bound to the wet wood. When he tried to move: the pain in his wrists brought sweat to his face. His hands were clenched together, bound at the wrists by thin, cutting wire.

He was helpless, unable to move, and deep inside Shurrock's Drift.

* * *

For Anne Morcomb, it proved to be a long, worrying morning. She had not gone to bed the previous night until almost two in the morning and then she had lain awake in her room, listening for the rasp of a taxi's wheels on the drive, heralding Eric's return. She had drifted off to sleep just before dawn, but was wide awake and out of bed by seven, feeling drugged with tiredness and anxiety.

She could not understand why Eric would have found it necessary to stay out; she had rung the flat several times, on the off-chance that he might have decided to stay in Newcastle rather than make the journey out to Sedleigh Hall, but there had been no reply. There was the possibility that he might have stayed in an hotel, but she thought it unlikely when the flat in Gosforth was available. At about eleven she rang the solicitor to the board, Mr Higgins, but he was unable to give her any information. He caught the sound of anxiety in her tone, however, and she explained that she was worried because in his state of health Eric should not be staying away from the Hall.

'He *is* a grown man,' old Higgins said sententiously. 'And more aware than anyone of his own health. I shouldn't worry: he'll have met someone, spent the night . . .' He coughed discreetly, as though he had just considered the possibility that Eric Ward might have spent the night with a woman other than Anne Morcomb. 'As I said, don't worry, he'll turn up, or get a message—'

'Do you think I should call the police?'

A note of alarm entered the solicitor's voice. 'Oh, my dear girl, positively not! It's *far* too early to be thinking of *that* sort of thing! Dear me, he rang you last night, didn't he?'

'Well, yes, he did,' Anne admitted. 'He couldn't ring from the office so he called me later, before he took a meal in Newcastle. He told me he'd arranged to meet someone—'

'Who?'

'A man called Kenton . . . an ex-colleague from his days in the police force.' Anne hesitated, unwilling to say more regarding the reasons for the meeting.

'Well, there you are, then,' Higgins chuckled. 'They'll have got to talking about the old days, you know the sort of thing men do in such circumstances. He'll turn up later this afternoon, believe me . . . he'll Just have stayed the night with this fellow Kenton. But as for calling the police, believe me, Anne, it's neither necessary nor wise. You don't want the story getting out that you'd called them out to look for your . . . friend, and then when he turns up . . . I mean, the *publicity* . . .'

Higgins was right, of course: it was foolish to let anxiety rob her of all sense of proportion. She took a cup of coffee, and tried to read, but felt the beginnings of a headache. In jeans and a windcheater she left the house, walked down to the Lower Farm and talked for a while with the tenant farmer's wife. It was lunch-time before she turned back to make her way across the fields, back to the Hall.

The earlier good weather had changed: storm clouds now scudded across the hills and the Cheviots were blanked out by mist. A spattering of rain came and she stood for a few minutes under a tree, looking out across the muddy field towards the Hall, thinking about her father, and the way she had met Eric Ward, and how she sometimes felt she would never really touch him, never reach into his mind and body in the way she desperately wanted to. He loved her, she knew that, but there were always the barriers he had erected, calling them honesty and realism. For her, all that was honest and realistic was bound up in him, she *needed* him, and if she were to lose him now she felt there would be little left to live for.

She thrust her hands deep into the pockets of her windcheater and began to walk again, ignoring the light rain that fell. It was a sobering thought, to have your life so bound up with another human being, to be so dependent upon another's love that nothing else could matter — not money, not land, perhaps not even life.

The rain increased in intensity; she had no scarf and her hair was quickly plastered to her head. She ignored it, plodding on, almost holding her breath as she came up past the fence to reach the spot where she would have a view of the driveway outside the Hall. She clenched her hands, prayed that he might be standing on the steps, watching for her, or that she might see him at the window, or that there might be a taxi in the drive.

She was doomed to disappointment.

She walked quickly up the drive and entered the Hall.

The middle-aged woman who worked as her secretary in the mornings was just leaving; she said there'd been no phone calls, no message from Eric. The disappointment and the nervousness felt like a lead weight in her breast and she rang down to say she would have no lunch; instead, she poured herself a whisky from the decanter, and stood staring out at the drive, her wet hair still plastered to her head. Only when she had finished the drink did she go to the bathroom on the first floor to dry her hair, and then she changed into a dress, inspected herself critically in the glass, told herself she'd end up like an old hag if she kept behaving in this ridiculous manner, and then, as she came out of her room and walked towards the top of the stairs, she heard one of the servants opening the front door. She felt the quick rush of excitement and relief; she hurried to the stairs, began to descend quickly, half laughing, and as she came to the bend she called out chidingly. 'Eric, don't you realize—'

But it wasn't Eric. The manservant stood there in the hallway staring up at her; the man beside him, shaking rain from his coat, was someone she had seen just once before, here at the Hall.

'It's Mr Kenton, madam,' the manservant said, and quietly walked away.

Kenton stood staring at her as she came down the stairs. It was possible her nervousness was communicated to him, her sudden fear palpable enough to raise echoes in the ex-policeman himself. He certainly seemed ill at ease, edgy, and his eyes did not meet hers, but shifted, shooting glances about him as though searching for something.

Or someone.

'I . . . er . . . I'm sorry. You'll be Miss Morcomb. We haven't exactly met, yet.'

He was extending a pudgy hand, stubby-fingered, broken-nailed. She stared at him and something in his face retreated; his mouth moved uneasily, and tiny wrinkles appeared around his eyes, cicatrices of doubt. 'Eric's not here,' she said, and the voice sounded unlike hers overlaid with strain.

'No?' He etched surprise into his voice and eyes, and looked around him again, vaguely, as though in a way he had not really expected Eric to be here. 'I thought . . . when he didn't show—'

'What?'

The eyes hardened, took courage, fixed on hers and she shrugged.

'I had an appointment to meet him, Miss Morcomb. Last evening. Up at the Prudhoe Street Mission. He didn't turn up. Or at least—'

'Yes?'

He blinked at the urgency in her voice. He ran the back of his hand across his cheek, wiping away a drop of rainwater

141

that had trickled down from his hair. 'Well, thing is, I was late. Didn't turn up for twenty minutes, or more. You see—' He hesitated, squinting doubtfully at her for a moment. 'You know all about this thing, don't you?'

Her knees suddenly felt weak. She walked across the hallway and entered the drawing-room. He followed her, a few paces behind. She stood in front of the window staring sightlessly at the rain-shrouded hills. Kenton remained behind her, shuffling uneasily. At last, quietly, she said, 'Svensson, you mean.'

'That's right,' he said in an eager, thick voice. 'I told Eric the bastard was alive; I got a trace on him on Tyneside whatever the narks like Bateman think. I had it set up, knew where he was hanging out, and I told Eric to meet me up at the top of Westgate Hill. But then something went wrong. I couldn't understand it, but I got word Svensson was on to me, flitting-like, so I had to make a check, it made me late, and when I got to the Prudhoe Street Mission, Eric wasn't there.' He hesitated, then added lamely, 'I guessed he'd got tired waiting, and had gone home. Come back here.'

Anne turned, trying to keep calm, fighting the panic that was rising in her throat, threatening to choke her. She held Kenton's piggy little eyes with her own, struggling to keep the anxiety out of her features. 'Eric didn't come back here last night.'

Dick Kenton frowned, seemed about to say something, then glanced at his watch. 'He . . . he told you he was meeting me?'

'He rang to tell me so, from Central Station.'

'He didn't come back — and he's not been in touch since?'

Anne shook her head, and Kenton consulted his watch again with a brief, puzzled shake of the head. 'I don't get it. I'd have thought he'd have been in touch with *me*, at least. I mean, I told him I was on to Svensson . . .'

His voice died away suddenly and Anne's legs began to shake. She turned away, poured herself a whisky, and when she looked at him he shook his head, glancing again at his watch as though suddenly anxious to be away.

'Where do you think Eric's gone, Mr Kenton?' Anne asked, and sipped her whisky, controlling the nervous shaking of her hand.

'Oh hell, I don't know, he'll turn up, maybe he's got some kind of lead. The fact is, Svensson's flown the coop from where he was hiding out, but I got some pretty good ideas about where . . .' Again he consulted his watch, then seemed to make up his mind. 'Look, don't worry about it. I'll get it sorted out. Leave it to me. I'm sure that . . .' The words died again on his lips, as though the thought that was in both their minds was not to be uttered.

He turned, began to walk to the door, and Anne put down her drink to follow him. He walked into the hallway, shrugging his heavy shoulders into his raincoat buttoning up its front fussily like a matron reluctant to go out in the rain, seemingly unwilling to leave Anne in her obvious, though controlled distress. He injected concern into his little eyes as he turned back to her, pushing his hands into his pockets. 'You . . . er . . . you get in touch with the police last night?'

Anne thought of Higgins's advice. She shook her head 'Do you think I should have done?'

Dick Kenton considered for a moment, then shrugged. 'Probably not: bit early to go jumping to any conclusions, even, when Svensson might be involved. But if this goes on —' He consulted his watch again and then nodded decisively. 'Okay, I got to be on my way. But look, I scribbled this number on a piece of paper. If anything transpires, you know where to get in touch with me, hey?'

She accepted the grubby slip of paper and he turned, began to walk towards the door. He opened it, stood framed in the doorway, peering out at the rain and then looked back to her. 'Like I said, if there's anything . . .'

The telephone rang. Anne ignored the ex-policeman and swung around, almost ran towards the phone in the hallway: She snatched it up eagerly, the name rushing out almost instinctively. 'Eric—'

The phone. was silent for an agonized five seconds, or more. The voice that then came, muffled, indistinct, was not Eric's, and it was the last voice in the world she wanted to hear.

'Listen. Don't speak, just listen . . . My name is Svensson. I have your friend Ward in a safe place. You can have him back . . . you listening to me?'

There was a brief pause, and Anne said, 'Now wait please—'

The voice cut across hers, brutally. *'You can have him back but it's going to cost you. Fifteen thousand pounds. Don't contact the police . . . and I want cash, used notes. You got five hours to raise it . . . or Ward's a dead man. Be clear about it: I got an old score to settle. But I'll take the money instead. I'll be ringing again this evening with instructions. If you got the money then, okay. If not, say goodbye to Eric Ward.'*

There was a click, the connection was broken with a rattling sound, and Anne Morcomb dropped the receiver from her nerveless fingers.

She was hardly aware of what had happened during the few minutes that had intervened. She was sure she had not fainted, but she had no recollection of what she had said or done; her mind had obviously blanked out for she found herself sitting in the drawing-room, with a freshly filled glass of whisky in her hand and Dick Kenton standing over her concernedly.

'Go on, drink it, take a stiff one, get it down you,' he was urging her.

She tried to comply, and the fierce spirit burned her tongue and her throat so that she coughed, spluttered, and could put the tears of panic in her eyes down to the effect of the whisky. Dick Kenton gripped her shoulder. 'That's better,' he said. 'Hell, you gave me a shock then; you all but dropped with the bloody phone. You all right now? Able to tell me?'

She was hardly able to see him through the blurred vision that affected her. 'Eric—'

'That was Eric?' he asked swiftly.

'No, no—'

'*Svensson,*' he almost snarled. 'It was Svensson, wasn't it? What did he have to say, the bastard?'

Anne's head dropped back helplessly as she leaned back in the chair. Her hand was shaking slightly and some whisky was spilled on her dress. 'He . . . he wants money. He says he has Eric and if I don't get him the money—'

'How much?'

'Fifteen thousand pounds.'

Dick Kenton made a harsh growling noise in his throat, part contempt, part admiration. 'As little as that . . . The bastard will settle for that little, knowing you can get it without too many questions asked, and without the bank blocking you too much. When does he want it?'

'He . . . he said he'd ring back tonight.'

'That means he'll want a swift drop of the money,' Kenton said with a malicious satisfaction. He paused for a few moments. 'He give any clue where he might have Eric?'

'He just said it was . . . it was a safe place.'

'The hell he did.' Dick Kenton stood back, walked nervously around the room for a few minutes. Then he came back, standing over her almost menacingly. 'Look, we got to get in touch with the police.'

'No, please—'

He overrode her mounting panic. 'Listen. I told you I got some ideas, maybe even can guess where Svensson is holding Eric, but it's too chancy for me to go chasing in, maybe let Svensson loose on Eric. Don't you understand? He's a wild bastard, he's got a score to settle, and even though he says he'll take the money we can't be *certain* he won't do for Eric as well, given the chance.'

'But he said I wasn't to contact the police—'

Kenton stood solidly in front of her. His piggy eyes were narrow and calculating, his mouth set hard, and unpleasant.

'I been chasing Svensson. He's trouble. He must know I've been watching him; if I *do* charge in on him now, like a blundering bull, he could just as easy stick a knife in Eric as smile. Whatever the bastard said to you on the phone, we got no choice. We *must* contact the police. They've got to handle this. There's no way I can deal with it alone, and you . . .'

His words died away, but the menace that lay behind them, for her and for Eric, remained like a tangible feeling in the air. He was right, of course: she had heard all about blackmail cases where, even after the money had been paid, the victim was either never discovered or was found dead. Kenton was an experienced ex-policeman; he knew the risks; even if he did have some ideas how to get to Eric and his captor he was just one man; He *needed* police support. Feebly she nodded her head. 'All right, if you say so, but for God's sake—'

He grunted in satisfaction, turned away, walked across the room. She opened her mouth to tell him there was a phone in the room but he was already stepping into the hallway, clearly not having noticed the drawing-room phone. The door was still open; she took another strong drink and leaned her head back helplessly, tears still gathering in her eyes, her heart still thudding almost painfully in her chest, and she listened to the one-sided conversation that drifted through to her from the hallway.

'Kenton . . . that's right, *Dick* Kenton . . . Oh, for God's sake . . . that's right, I want to speak to Bateman . . . no, no one else, he's the brass I want . . .'

It was all so unreal, it could not be happening to her and to Eric. The fears were so different, so changed: it had been the surgery, his too early return to work, and then his fall. But now . . .

'That's right, I said *kidnapped!* What the hell do you think for? Money, for God's sake . . .'

The voice would come again tonight, the hateful, muffled tones of the man who was prepared to kill Eric Ward. For just fifteen thousand pounds. It was a ludicrously small sum, to set against a life. She would willingly pay it, to get Eric back. But Kenton was right: to pay it would not guarantee his safety. The police would know what to do; with Kenton, they would know what to do.

The conversation from the hallway was even more disjointed now. Kenton appeared to be arguing about something, but his silences were more protracted, as though he was listening to proposals being put to him by Detective-Superintendent Bateman. He did not appear to be entirely in agreement with them, and at one point began to argue strongly: only to lapse into silence again. Finally, she heard him say, almost angrily, 'All right then, it's your game, and I'll go along with it. Yes, all right. But there's a risk, believe me, and if that's the case . . . well, all right, I'll go along with it.'

The phone was replaced with a clatter. There was a short silence and Anne could visualize the stocky, pudgy form of Dick Kenton standing in the hallway, glaring angrily at the inanimate object he had just put down, transferring his anger to it, rather than bringing it back with him into the room. Anne brushed the back of her hand across her eyes as she heard Kenton come back into the room. He stood looking at her uncertainly, and then pointed to the whisky decanter. 'You mind?'

He was tense; nervous. She nodded abstractedly and watched him while he poured himself a drink. 'What did the police say?'

'Bateman. Arrogant bastard. Wants to play it his way.' Kenton took a swallow of whisky and grimaced. 'Still, he's a hard man, and knows his business. You can get rusty too, away from the force.'

'So what's going to happen?' Anne asked.

'It's Bateman's game. He's going to handle the situation. I'm to meet him, give him what information I got, and he'll use his own contacts to suss out the whole thing. We got a few hours yet to set up an operation.'

'Do you . . . do you know where Eric is being held?'

'I got a pretty good idea,' Kenton said grimly. He finished the whisky in one long gulp and grimaced again, shook his head slightly. 'Anyway, I got to go.'

'What do I do?'

Dick Kenton hesitated. 'It's not the way I'd play it . . .'

'What do I *do?*'

'Two things. It's not my way, but Bateman is scared we might foul it all up, or maybe he thinks the grabbing of the money will expose Svensson earlier. He wants you to get the fifteen thousand, then get back here, stay close to the phone. Don't make any calls yourself, because all it would need would be for Svensson to call and get an engaged signal: he's crazy enough to think anything, like you was calling the police.'

'That's all?'

Kenton nodded. 'Get the money . . . and wait. Me, I'll get my instructions from Bateman, and do all I can to help.' He smiled suddenly, and wolfishly. Funny thing, you know, I'd like to get my hands on that bastard personal, now, like. There was times in the old days . . . it's just like they were back.'

Anne stared at him, a cold feeling in her stomach. Dick Kenton, in spite of the anger he had felt in his conversation with Bateman, was beginning to enjoy himself. And it was not just the feeling of a hunter, she suspected: Kenton was hoping, and expecting to use personal violence. To hurt a man, badly. Eric had once said something to her, hinted at Dick Kenton's reputation for mindless violence when he had been in the force. It had been why he had been forced to leave.

Now, it was as though he felt licensed to use such violence again, and was looking forward to the opportunity.

* * *

It had been his father's watch, a piece bought late in life, a source of pride and something the sentimentalist in Eric

148

had clung to, a visible reminder of a man he had really only got to know when he was close to the end of his life. It was useless to him now, the watch, useless because he had been unable to wind it, bound as he was, and useless too because there was not enough light in the drift to reflect the luminous hands of the dial.

Even so, the stirrings of his stomach, and his body clock itself told him that he must have been lying here in the arched tunnel for perhaps twenty-four hours. He had slept fitfully for several periods, but most of the time he had lain cold and shivering, feeling helpless and sorry for himself and searching for answers that would lie in the past as well as the present, but the questions were probably the wrong ones, the conclusions inconclusive.

All he really knew was that he was buried deep in Shurrock's Drift, that he had been left alone all night and probably most of the next day, and that soon, very soon, Svensson must come for him.

There had been a time in the cold, wet darkness, in what he guessed was the early period of the morning, when he had doubted Svensson's return, and the child in him had cried out at the fear of being left alone to die, unheard and unseen in the darkness of the drift. But later there was the realization that it would not be that way. The hatred Svensson felt for him, mistaken or not, based on his mother's death or not, was too deep and too fierce for it to be satisfied at a distance, with Eric lying in the tunnel and Svensson miles away.

Besides, he was still alive. Svensson had attacked him at the wheelhouse: he could easily have killed him there. The fact that Eric was still alive, and incarcerated in the drift, meant that there was some purpose he yet had to serve for Svensson. The man would come back: Eric Ward knew it.

The realization drew him, finally, away from the spinning, wandering, dreaming unrealities his mind had led him into: he became more conscious of the dull ache in his arms, the fact that there was little pain in his numbed wrists when he moved them now, and the knowledge that if he did nothing to protect himself from Svensson's return there was no other person who would be available to do so. He had phoned Anne yesterday, but only she knew of his failure to return to Sedleigh Hall. There was Kenton, but he would merely assume Eric had not turned up, though it was likely that his need to boost his earnings from Eric Ward would eventually lead to his contacting Anne.

Eventually, only eventually.

His wrists were slippery during the afternoon. It would be blood, he guessed, but there was no pain. He considered that strange: it was as though the wire cutting into his wrists had no longer the power to hurt, for his brain refused to accept the signals. Similarly, the scratching that had plagued the nerve ends behind his eyes was also gone: his body had enough to cope with and in the dank darkness he needed no drugs to combat that old pain.

Several times he attempted to scramble to his feet but failed; he was lying awkwardly against the curving stone wall of the tunnel but when he attempted to obtain purchase with his feet he merely slipped in the mud. It was several hours before he thought about that mud: in the close, cold blackness his mind had a disturbing habit of veering off into irrelevancies, disorientated in a way he had briefly experienced when the surgical bandages had been constraining his vision. This was far worse, with regard to discomfort, the pain and the helplessness of his situation. After the surgery, at least he had had freedom of movement; now, there was no relief.

Even so, the mud did not draw his attention for a long time. He had concentrated on the water; the maddening persistence of its dripping played on his tortured nerves both by its regularity, the sound thunderous in his head for some periods, and by the tantalizing nature of its sound. He was thirsty, he could have drunk it if he had been able to reach it, and if he had not been gagged. Not that it would have been fit to slake his thirst, slimy with mud.

But mud meant earth, soil, the thick slithering of his shoes told him so. The drift, in spite of its age and disuse, should not normally have been subject to thick mud. The ancient tracks running into the drift were still there, he knew: he had seen them earlier, at the entrance. But now, as he stretched out his foot he could not feel the iron: instead, there was only the wet slime and then something soft. Earth. A pile of earth.

There had been a collapse in the tunnel.

He had a sudden, flashing picture of Svensson dragging his inert body into the drift. In his place, Eric would have gone deep into Shurrock's Drift, turning into one of the side passages that would have appeared, effectively preventing the sound of a man's shouts escaping from the tunnel. There should have been no need for a gag. It was a clumsy contrivance, as likely to choke a man as to silence him; it would have been a late decision, perhaps, one not properly thought out.

It meant that Eric Ward had not been concealed deeply in the drift because Svensson had found it too dangerous to go further. Dangerous, when faced by the collapse of the old drift wall.

It accounted for the baulk of timber to which he was bound. Gingerly, Eric explored it with numbed fingers. It was old, wet, decayed and splitting under the eroding water dripping from the roof. But what had been its purpose? It could have been an original prop, used to support the roof but that was unlikely: here the walls were stone, the tunnel was *lined* in part, shored up against collapse but a collapse had taken place.

The timber had been a later, temporary prop, perhaps set up after the drift had been closed, while engineers were still working in there, removing equipment. But from its present angle it was clear that its days as a support had been numbered: it had snapped under the weight, or slipped at its base, years ago. Svensson must have realized it, maybe had even been quite maliciously deliberate in using it as a chaining post. Too wild an attempt to escape could have resulted in Eric Ward's death through a roof fall.

And then Eric knew what he must do.

First he tried to bring life back into his fingers and hands: the flexing of his fingers, the pressure of fingertip against fingertip did indeed eventually bring back life, but with the increased flow of blood came the pain. He gritted his teeth and struggled on, and as he did so sought with deliberation for some purchase for his feet. It took him almost an hour, and the rag in his mouth was a hard ball, sourness dry in his throat as he felt the earth and mud balling under his foot, collecting against the rails hidden inches below the surface. He pushed and stamped and the mud was thick, the earth giving him purchase as the stones that had fallen from above were clamped together. Only then did he raise himself until his forearms were pressed against the beam and, on his knees, he took a long, deep breath, and thrust hard and suddenly against the baulk of timber.

Nothing happened.

He tried again, angrily, but the timber was unresponsive, the only sound being his own harsh breathing and the slithering of his shoes in the mud. He rested then for a while, waiting, thinking, conscious of the pain in his wrists and chest but dismissing it, concentrating on what he had to do. Then he returned to his task.

This time he did not waste his effort. He did not know whether he would be able to move the baulk of timber, but it was not to be done by wild, angry thrusts. If he could have got his shoulder beneath the timber he would have stood a better chance, but it was only his forearms he could trust to; now he leaned and pushed, strongly, steadily, and in short bursts. He needed to conserve his energy; it could take a long time.

As he worked his mind drifted to the past, to his young days as a policeman. He had prided himself on his fitness then; that same pride had made him keep in shape of recent years. It had been a way of persuading himself that his body had not really changed, in spite of the inhibition of his eyesight problems. He was glad now, as the sweat dripped from him in spite of the cold dankness of the tunnel, and he flexed the lean muscles of his forearms, pushing, arching his back desperately, bringing all the power he could bear from his cramped position, feeling the mud slither beneath his feet, fighting to retain sufficient purchase to throw his kneeling weight against the beam.

Until, finally, there was another, foreign sound.

It held an eerie note in the long dark tunnel of the drift. A soft groan, whispering in the roof above, sending a flutter into the tunnel like a skittering bird against the stone. He stopped, listened, sweating profusely, streaked with mud and grime, and the sound came again, the settling of old earth and ancient stone, pressures and powers and strengths that had been building up for years, waiting for their own time to demonstrate their crushing abilities and stirring now, testing those abilities in a long, slow groan. Eric's blood was pounding as he leaned heavily against the baulk of timber, and this time there was not merely the soft groaning: the timber moved, slipped sideways for a fraction of an inch and the walls murmured to him that their sleep was over, and they were alive again.

At that, Eric rested his head against the timber itself. He had moved it a little; the pressures from the roof would mean that he could move it again. But not yet, not too soon, and carefully.

His blood slowed, and he slept for a little while and there was a confusion, of stalls on the market place along the Quayside, a narrow street along Eldon Square; Philip Scarn stood astride a recumbent figure, a woman, bleeding in a flat in Byker, but the faces were blurred, his vision limited, as he tried to tear aside the veils of glaucoma, affecting sight and resolution and logic.

When he woke, it was with a start.

There was a rustling sound in the blackness, the movement of something small, careful, furry. He felt the scrape of teeth against his shoe and kicked out in sudden panic. Rats would live down here in the drift: and he was alive and still, and they were investigating. Bile rose in his throat but he could not get rid of it; he fought the heavings of his stomach because he knew it could end in his own death if he were sick now. He focused his mind on the timber, felt it against his forearms, *saw* it in his mind's eye in the darkness, classified it as an antagonist to be overcome and conquered. He strained again, and rested; strained, and once again there was the slight shift, the movement, and the trembling excitement of rock that had not moved in thirty years.

He was surrounded by immense power and some of it now seemed to flow down into him. He was no longer aware of the cold and the pain; instead, a light-headed intoxication took his mind, as he knew the drift willed him to create even if it were only the destruction of what man had done to the glen and the hill that held the drift. He pushed and strained and the timber moved again, there was a shower of dirt on his face, and beyond the timber something fell with a cracking sound from the roof itself. He lay back, breathing heavily through a nose half blocked with suffocating dirt, and the euphoria left him as suddenly as it had gripped him. He began to shake, pressed his head against his hands, feeling the blood that streaked them touch his cheek, slippery, wet.

And he heard the other, distant sound.

It was light, far off, and for a moment inexplicable. It echoed faintly in the dark air, drifting softly through the hollows of the tunnel, losing itself against the roof. Eric raised his head, straining to catch the sound again, and there was something odd about it, sharp, light, a piercing sound that was metamorphosed in flight, dissected and broken up until it lost its form against the bouncing back of its echoes. He had heard the sound before, many times, but could not now make out its quality or its cadence. But finally, as the echoes lost their strength for a few seconds, and the noise became uncertain, irregular, Eric knew it for what it was.

The sound of a man whistling. Svensson was returning into the drift.

Eric scrambled with his feet, found fresh purchase and took a deep breath. He curled his fingers against the wet, split timber and closed his eyes. The whistling noise, still corrupted by distance and echo, was less faint now and he knew he had only minutes to go before Svensson came into the last curve of the drift, and he pressed his forearms against the baulk and pushed hard.

There was no response. Where he had felt movement there was immobility; where the walls had chuckled menacingly at him, moving as he strained their support, now there was only silence except for the cutting edge of the man's whistle, sharp against his nerves and panic. He pushed again, but the timber resisted him with a new stubbornness: it had lain here for almost thirty years and had regained confidence in its own strength. He felt as though it were alive, and fury hammered in the blood of his temples, his neck corded with effort as he thrust again, scrabbling with his toes, straining the muscles of his forearms against the wet timber. Nothing moved; the roof was silent, and the whistling had stopped to change into a mocking gibberish that was growing louder, words dancing confused in the darkness, except it was no longer dark, there was a faint ghost of light deep down the tunnel and he knew that he had failed, he was too late.

The air was grey now, a stain upon the blackness, the first marking of a photographic plate with images and realities. The dank darkness that had been suffocating him now seemed to have been more like a benison, and he desperately longed for its return as he thrust violently against the timber baulk, feeling the blood trickle along his wrists as the wire cut deep, searching for bone.

The faint light grew in intensity, until it was a swinging, dancing luminescence that hurt his eyes, sent fantastic images whirling against the black wet stone of the tunnel, and conjured up fantasies of shadow as Eric struggled with the stubborn baulk and the drift waited silently, ponderous, unresentful of the intrusion of the light and the heavy step and the song of the man who came down the tunnel seeking for Eric Ward.

The incongruity of the words, the triumph of the song came to Eric as he desperately thrust against the baulk. He had heard the words roared drunkenly on a Saturday night; they still came out of the pubs and the back alleys and St James's Park and the music hall. Svensson had won; he knew it, and he sang softly, and contentedly and ironically.

'Howway, lads, you should've seen 'em gannin' . . .'

The light was glancing off the roof and Eric could see the black stain of blood on his wrists. He thrust against the timber again, and thought he felt it move. The steps came closer, the light grew brighter, and the baulk shivered, the roof setting up again its own light groaning as a counterpoint to the man's voice as he came around the curve, the flashlight dancing and flickering and leaping ahead of him.

'Gannin' along the Scotswood Roooad, ter see the Blaydon Races . . .'

Then the light was playing full on Eric Ward and the song stopped and the beam lifted, inspected Eric as he lay there, held the wrists and the baulk of timber in its glare, and the voice came chuckling, menacingly. 'Oh aye, and what we been up to here then, hey, bonny lad?'

The tunnel whispered in answer, and the light wavered, dashed a suspicious flash against the roof, and as the whisper echoed in the passageway, the beam fixed Eric again. 'Right, you bastard,' the man said, and Eric thrust with one final desperate heave against the baulk and the timber. slipped sideways, there was one long demonic screeching as stone tore at stone and the noise turned to thunder, crashing and rumbling into the depths of the old drift mine until the roof came crashing down about them in a choking, rubble-loaded cloud of dust and earth and stone.

* * *

The thunder echoed and complained interminably, rumbling into distant new caverns underground, sending tremors of sound into long disused workings, realigning rock and streams of percolating water, seeking out new beds, settling into new patterns, until it faded, to be replaced with a different noise, an aching, thudding noise that was inside Eric Ward's head.

It was several minutes before he was able to appreciate where he was, momentarily stunned by the fall of rock and stone, pinned by the broken baulk of timber that had been shattered in the fall. When he regained his senses he realized he was racked with a bout of coughing: the constraint of the gag had been torn from his face and he had almost automatically spat out the wad of rag. His hands were still bound, but the timber to which he was still attached was moveable, perhaps three feet in length, and he found he could curl his fingers around the end of it: For a moment he thought of trying to ease the binding wire over the end of the timber, but soon realized it was impossible: the wire would not slip and he would succeed only in further shredding of the skin and flesh at his wrists.

He lay still then, for a long time, and listened.

The thunder in the tunnel had died away and so had the noise in his head. He was faintly dizzy and felt sick, but the blackness, though thick with dust and oppressive, still allowed him to breathe. There was no light, no human sound, though distantly he heard the squeal of a frightened, dangerous rat.

He knew he would have to move. It was possible the tunnel was now completely blocked; if so, he was imprisoned here until he died. He had no illusions about that. His captor would have come alone, and Eric had insufficient strength left to dig his way out past any major fall. His only hope was that the collapse had been localized, and the exit from the drift was still open.

He lay there, listening, but there was no sound other than the soft slither of earth, and after a while he started to move, to struggle to his feet.

Every muscle in his body seemed concerned to complain, to demonstrate its displeasure at the treatment to which it had been subjected, and Eric groaned quietly. The sound seemed hung in the air, alien, a light echo drifting away from him in the darkness, and he forced himself up to his knees, his wrists still bound to the piece of timber. He stayed like that on his knees for almost two minutes, waiting until his head cleared and his breathing came more easily and then, with caution, he tried to stand upright.

The blackness around him was intense and he could see nothing, but the roof had not collapsed and he was able to move, hopefully in the direction of the entrance to the drift. He knew the earth and stone was piled in uneven heaps all about him as a result of the fall and he moved cautiously, stumbling nevertheless as he groped his way forward.

And then he stopped, stood stock still, as he heard the other groan, the second echo, and the sound of someone else moving, scrabbling against earth and rock, scrambling painfully to his feet.

'*Svensson!*'

The name hissed from his lips, a sibilant whisper in the blackness. It soughed against the roof, sighed along the black corridor of the drift, and the noise ahead of him stopped. The man stood there, like himself blind in the tunnel, but between Eric and the exit from the drift. But now they were equal. A sharp excitement scored through Eric's veins, adrenalin pumping strength into him as he realized that the handicap he had suffered was one they now both laboured under in the blackness of the tunnel. He said the name again, viciously.

'*Svensson!* I'm here; I can hear you — but can you hear this?'

The piece of timber was still bound to his hands; his fingers clasped its end and he swished it viciously in the air, sending a light, dangerous sound sighing through the tunnel. Exultation gripped him; he was armed, Svensson would still be dazed, and Eric Ward wanted revenge. He swung the timber again, violently, and he heard rock and stone tumble only feet away as a heavy body was launched in his direction.

The blackness saved him. He felt fingers grasping at his shoulder and he swung his arms, brought the timber crashing against a muscular arm and then for a moment he was free again, only to smell that familiar, stale beer odour once more as his captor lurched for him again, hands outstretched in the blackness. He felt himself gripped by the shoulders, and then hands were scrabbling for his throat; he twisted, thudding the timber upwards and heard the crunch of bone. He struck again and the hands fell away, the man was backing into the tunnel and Eric followed him, wild with rage, swinging the timber pinioned to his wrists.

'Ward—'

The word was cut off, turned into a grunt of pain as the blow took him across the chest. Eric swung again and felt the blow slide upwards, half-deflected by a protecting arm, only to strike hard against the side of the man's head. The grunt of pain was muffled, there was a snorting sound and a scurry of falling earth and stone, and Eric heard the sound of a heavy body falling backwards. There was one more, light groan, and then only a slow, laboured breathing.

Eric groped forward carefully, the timber extended in front of him. The excitement that had gripped him was fading now, draining away with the sense of danger. Some eight feet from where he had lain there was a pile of broken rock; he struck it with his foot and fell, scoring his arm painfully, but as he lay there with his heart pounding he became aware of a softness under his fingers that was not earth, but flesh.

He explored tentatively. It was the upper part of a man's body, a fleshy face, light stubble. He felt hair, a sticky wetness and he turned, slipped his numb, bleeding fingers against the man's shirt, seeking life. After a few moments he picked up the faint flutter of a heartbeat and he sat up, checking with his hands and feet for purchase before he rose. Svensson was still alive, and the exit from Shurrock's Drift was no longer barred.

He staggered away from the inert body of the man who had bound him to the baulk of timber and began to make his way along the tunnel.

It was a nightmare journey in the blackness. He blundered along like an owl in daylight, colliding with the walls, stumbling over broken rubble and earth, falling to his ragged knees in the wet, slippery mud and never certain that he was moving in the right direction, never certain he would breathe clean air again.

* * *

He had no idea how long the journey took. He fell heavily at one point and his mouth was covered in soft, clinging earth so that he was forced to sit there, panting, spitting the dirt from his mouth. He crawled on his hands and knees for some distance, slow, painful movements, before he was able to brace himself again, rise to his feet to continue his stumbling progress, two hands against the broken wall of the tunnel, fingers gripping the trailing timber still wired painfully to his wrist. His imagination began to play tricks with him: he felt that the clogging atmosphere was changing, there was a new sweetness in the air, a freshness that was missing in the dust-laden tunnel behind him. And then perhaps it was not imagination after all as he thought he also detected a lightness in the tunnel, the kind of halo he had dreaded in his illness but now something to quicken his pulse. The floor of the drift seemed less strewn with rubble, and he was able to splash along with the feel of an old rail track under his feet. Then he knew the air *was* less tainted with dust, there was a change in atmosphere and light, and he knew he was nearing the entrance to Shurrock's Drift.

Two minutes later there were stars above his head and he could dimly discern the moon riding among dark, ponderous clouds that scudded heavily against the sky. He stared upwards, taking in great gulps of air, and waited as the tension eased in his body and his pulse began to return to normal. He tried to raise his hands, run the back of one hand against his eyes and the timber waved ludicrously above his head.

He stepped forward, swaying and lurching, but feeling stronger every moment as a cool night breeze whispered in his face: He reached the broken railings, gripped the iron with his hands and dragged himself through the rusted opening. He blinked, looked about him, uncertain of himself, disorientated once more. He could not see well in the darkness in spite of the moonlight: long shadows from the broken wheelhouse were cast over the open ground and all was silent about him. Nevertheless, with a slow prickling feeling at the base of his spine he realized he was not alone.

For a few moments he stood there puzzled, blinking, unable to focus properly. Then, gradually, he made out the two dark shapes that stood at the far side of the clearing outside the drift. Beyond the iron loading circle and to one side of the old dumpers there were two cars, one stationed just a few yards from the other: they sat there silently and menacingly, watching, waiting.

The blood began to pound in Eric's head; names surged through his mind — perhaps Svensson hadn't been alone, Scarn, Reilly, O'Connor . . . He took a hesitant step forward but there was no sound, no movement from the cars. He began to walk forward, raising his hands and then suddenly there was an impression in his mind, there had been a movement in the car to the right, a window being wound down, a head emerging. Someone was peering towards him across the intervening thirty yards. Eric stopped, puzzled, and then the voice came: high, light, scared.

'*Dick?*'

Eric Ward stood stock still as visions and questions and answers surged all around him and he struggled to make sense of it all in a brain clouded with pain and incomprehension. And then, at last, in an understanding anger. He had only those few moments, however, before, nightmarishly, the headlights of the car glowed briefly, then flickered on to flash a dazzling brilliance against his eyes, holding him in a searing glare of light. A woman screamed as though to match his own surprise, then it was drowned in the thunder of the car engine roaring into life. There was a violent clash of gears, a screeching sound that tore at his nerve ends and the headlights were moving, swinging erratically towards him, surging forward like a wild predator.

* * *

The rest was confusion and noise and violent reaction.

The car roared down on him and it could only have been feet from him before he moved. For a second his muscles refused to respond to the command of his brain; he remained rooted to the spot and then the reaction came. He hurled himself sideways in the automatic rolling response he had learned long ago in his police training. His left shoulder hit the ground, and though he rolled, the breath was still punched out of him, the timber thudding against his ribs. He felt the wind of the car as it roared past him, smelled oil and exhaust fumes and then he was on his knees, hardly able to move until he saw the brake lights gleaming red in the darkness, the car sliding, swinging, turning, until the headlights were pinning him again and it came charging in once more to hammer him into oblivion.

He staggered to his feet, raising his arms, but the light was so bright, lancing into him, and he knew he was unable to run, it was all over, pain and exhaustion and the tensions of the last hours had taken their toll on him. He stood there, weaving drunkenly, helpless. There was a high screaming sound again and the headlights wavered uncertainly before swinging violently to one side, the car twisting out of control, rocking as it bore down on him. And then, with a rush, it was past him, tyres squealing in protest as the car skidded, sliding at an angle for the walls of the old wheelhouse.

The car smashed into the wall at an angle with an explosion of sound that echoed around the clearing. Part of the wall collapsed, crushing the bonnet of the vehicle and the engine roared once more, crazily, before dying abruptly. An unearthly silence seemed to fill the clearing; the headlight on the near side still glared, whitening the destroyed walls of the wheelhouse, and as Eric staggered forward he saw movement inside the car. Someone was at the driving-wheel, sitting up slowly, one hand raised to the head.

He quickened his step, suddenly conscious again of the wire cutting into his wrists and made his way towards the car, where the door hung half torn from its hinges. He dragged at its edge, pulling it wide open and it screeched a complaint as the three-feet-long broken timber banged against the metal.

There were two women in the car. In the passenger seat Anne Morcomb was sprawled sideways. Her right hand was still fiercely clenched on the wheel; she had wrenched the car across from its murderous course and saved Eric Ward's life. Her eyes were closed, her lips half open, a smear of blood across her mouth.

Even as Eric stared at her the other woman moved. She was reaching for the glove compartment. He stood there foolishly, watching her as she dragged open the compartment and then the moonlight broke through, glinting on the small screwdriver that she suddenly jerked forward. She held its point against Anne Morcomb's throat in a gesture that was a compound of fear and defiance.

'*Don't come near me!*'

Her wild glare was fixed on Eric and the timber in his hand and there was panic and hatred in the glance. Eric Ward stood there, staring at her, and he realized at last what must have happened, knew how it had all come about, and he knew who it was who was lying in the rubble of Shurrock's Drift.

He shook his head slowly, leaned forward.

'*Don't come near me, or I'll shove this into her neck!*' The silence lengthened about them, broken only by the slow ticking sound of cooling metal. Eric leaned against the door wearily, and shook his head again. 'Put it down,' he said in a quiet voice. 'Put it down, Dorothy. It's all over now.'

And in a little while the defiance in her eyes died.

* * *

'You've caused me a great deal of inconvenience, Mr Ward,' Detective-Superintendent Bateman announced. He sat there in a dark grey suit of good cut, and his tone was sombre but polite, probably inhibited by the surroundings in which he found himself at Sedleigh Hall. Anne had already coolly offered him a glass of sherry, which he had declined with a certain stiffness, but the belligerence of his earlier attitude when he had interviewed Eric at his office was noticeably absent. It was clear that Bateman was now inclined to be more circumspect in his dealings with people whose suggestions might perhaps reach persons of standing in the county.

'Yes, a great deal of inconvenience. It would have been more helpful and sensible, and certainly less dangerous, if you had believed me in the first place.'

'I can't say that you were particularly convincing,' Eric replied, 'nor all that communicative. If you'd told me more at the time—'

'I saw no reason to take you into police confidence completely, simply because you'd once been in the force,' Bateman said in a cold voice. 'I went as far as I needed to and it should have been enough. I *told* you Svensson was dead. You chose to disbelieve me.'

'I was given other information.'

'From *Kenton!* Well, the less said about *that* piece of gullibility the better,' Bateman sneered. 'The fact is, we have been carrying out an investigation into corruption in the construction world for the last ten years. The trials of seven years ago when a few councillors and building contractors were finally nailed didn't end it all. There are still certain local politicians and a few professional men . . . however, I won't go into that. The thing is, when we heard Scarn was coming back north to Tyneside we weren't displeased. He had been on the fringe of the scandals ten years ago but was forced out by a bigger fish we've not yet managed to net — a man who since then has, shall we say, diversified.'

'Johnston O'Connor?'

Bateman smiled thinly. 'The same. We had a feeling Scarn's return might put some pressure on O'Connor, cause a few worms to emerge. And if you hadn't interfered—'

In the background Anne Morcomb stirred and Eric looked at her. There was a small scar on her upper lip, the result of the crash into the wheelhouse, but it would fade soon, together with the memories.

'We always knew Reilly was closely involved with O'Connor, and suspected there was some link through him between Scarn and O'Connor. We *guessed* the link might be Cindy Jackson. And we were working on the basis that if they were all left alone, and Scarn started needling O'Connor, things might happen.'

'Like the murder of a young girl,' Eric said quietly.

Bateman's face tightened. 'That was as much your doing as anyone's. I've told you before. Cindy Jackson had worked in Scarn's office in the old days. Reilly moved in to live with her and she began to slip information on Scarn's tenders to him; he passed it on to O'Connor. Nothing too serious in her book but it led to the collapse, essentially, of Scarn's business. Later, Reilly recruited the girl to O'Connor, put her on the game.'

'Scarn didn't know about her involvement, and neither did I.'

'That's not the point. When you started asking questions — around — and were known to be Scarn's lawyer — and actually visited the girl, O'Connor, always a man to protect his back, ordered Reilly to warn her to keep her mouth shut. But when Reilly went around to do just that he found a watch had been placed on the flat. By *you*.'

'I—'

'He gave your night watchman a going-over, then, his blood up, he went to talk to Cindy. He claims he didn't intend to kill her, just to warn her, but things got out of hand. He was always a violent man — this time he went too far.'

'Have you arrested him?' Anne asked.

'He was taken last night in Northallerton. Never run far, these Geordies. All the same; stick to the North-East.'

'That's what I thought, about Svensson.' Eric said in a tight voice.

Bateman glared at him for a moment, then twisted his mouth unpleasantly. 'That's as may be, but *I* still told you the man was dead. The man *you* saw in Byker, outside Cindy's flat, was just a passer-by sheltering from the rain. But you wouldn't listen.' He was silent for a moment, clearly resentful that Eric had disregarded his warnings, but not inclined to pursue the matter further. 'Still, I'm here now to tell you that I'll need formal statements from you about Kenton and Dorothy Farnon . . . Kenton looked half gone when we finally hauled him out of Shurrock's Drift but he's recovered well enough. Cracked skull and broken ribs from the thumping you gave him, but he'll be fit and well by the time he and Dorothy Farnon stand trial.' He glanced around the room, appreciative of his surroundings. 'It was all about envy, really. Envy, and greed.'

'How do you mean?'

'They were both corrupted by their experiences, lack of prospects; seeing you, and thinking they deserved better than they had . . . It seems the day you went to London to talk to Philip Scarn, Kenton was down there too, being interviewed for a job he *didn't* get. He was angry, depressed . . . and he got drunk. It was as he was going for his train—'

'That he caught sight of me,' Eric supplied. 'While I couldn't see him.'

'Precisely. And what *did* he see? A man more successful than he, yet one who'd been junior to him in the force and who'd been compelled to resign because of illness. Yet you'd since become a solicitor and . . . forgive me . . . attached to a wealthy young woman.' Bateman hesitated. 'It wasn't premeditated, he insists on that. Says he was drunk, envious, disappointed by his failure, and he just barged into you on the steps above the underpass. A combination of his own disappointments and your *apparent* success, a well-dressed solicitor visiting London for a business conference . . .'

'And afterwards?' Anne asked.

'He claims it just sort of grew. He didn't tell Dorothy Farnon about the incident immediately. But the accident, so-called, was still on his mind a few days later. He had a few cans of brown ale inside him, was brooding over your good fortune and his ill luck, and he took it a step further. He made a threatening phone call. A joke, he argues. But Mrs Farnon caught him at it, told him he was a malicious fool, likely to get into trouble for nothing. And that's when it changed.'

'With her intervention?'

'Your foolishness, more like,' Bateman suggested sourly. 'You went around to Keelman's Bridge to seek Kenton's help to find a dead man. That's when it germinated. The seed was already there: you just gave it life by suggesting a name to them. Kenton was scared when you arrived — he thought you knew he'd made that first phone call. Then he was taken aback — and Dorothy Farnon was quick to see the possibilities.'

'She worked it out?' Eric asked.

'You gave the idea form and substance and she had the drive and intelligence to push Kenton into it: convince you Svensson was still alive, and scare Miss Morcomb enough to make her hand over some money. Nothing too fancy; nothing too elaborate; and not too much money. Just enough, he says, to enable them to buy a small business.' Bateman sniffed. 'Can't see it would have bought them much these days.'

Anne rose, folded her arms tightly, and walked across the room towards the window. She stared out over the meadow for a few moments. 'The phone calls . . . they were horrible.'

'Dorothy Farnon made him keep them to a minimum. He disguised his voice and made sure he was actually *at* the Hall, visibly not making them, when they came through.

167

And it kept things warm while they worked out a plan to extract the money. But you rushed them a bit—'

'It was after you told me about Cindy Jackson's death,' Eric said woodenly.

'All right, but you rushed them. Kenton had to hurry to set it up after your visit the second time to Keelman's Bridge, and the planning got a bit loose. He arranged the meeting at the Prudhoe Street Mission, gave the kid the note for you, and drove out to Shurrock's Drift ahead of you. He'd previously sussed the place out, as a possibility.'

Eric nodded, recalling his second visit to Keelman's Bridge. 'I think I saw him after he'd returned from a visit there. He was tired, his jacket was dirty—'

'No doubt,' Bateman interrupted, his pale, unblinking eyes unemotional. 'Anyway, once he'd attacked you and stuck you in the drift, the next problem was to get the money out of Miss Morcomb.'

'Dorothy Farnon worked that out?'

'She did. Pretty fool proof, too. Kenton's job was to come here to Sedleigh Hall, alarm Miss Morcomb, plant fears about your safety.'

Anne shuddered at the recollection. 'It wasn't difficult. I was already scared to hell.'

'Quite so.' Bateman smoothed his stiffly brushed hair as though to reassure himself of the realities in the face of female weakness. 'The additional thing he had to be certain of was that he was in the Hall when "Svensson's" blackmail call came through.'

Anne hesitated. 'But then, and earlier—'

Eric had already worked it out. 'Kenton had pre-recorded the message. Dorothy Farnon had made a little investment — a music centre with a taping device. You told me Kenton kept watching the time when he was with you, looking at his watch. The timing was crucial. He'd fixed a precise time with Dorothy; at the arranged time she'd ring and when she was sure you were on the line she switched on the tape. To all intents and purposes you were listening to Svensson — who would allow you no interruption — at the very time Kenton just *happened* to be at the Hall. And on this last occasion, importantly, available to help, assist you in making a decision when you were shaken, confused — and there to make certain you *were* shaken enough to be deceived.'

'So the call to police headquarters, the one made from the hallway—'

'Was never made.' A touch of colour stained Bateman's oily skin. 'He simply didn't dial the number. There was no call to headquarters, no conversation with me or any other policeman. It was simply a way of gaining your confidence, allaying any suspicions you might have had. It may all have *sounded* realistic, but . . . in any case, I would never have suggested you drew out the money, Miss Morcomb. The police simply don't work like that.'

Anne shook her head ruefully. 'I was confused. In a pretty bad way if the truth be told. I just couldn't think straight. And when Kenton phoned later, told me Dorothy Farnon would be calling to pick me up with the money, to go to the police rendezvous, I simply didn't question it. I was stupid.'

'Confused,' Eric insisted softly. In the way he had been shaken the last time at Keelman's Bridge when he failed to become suspicious of the reactions of Kenton and Dorothy Farnon.

Anne shook her head. 'Even so, I should have realized . . . the way Kenton was so nervous when he came to the house that afternoon. The way he kept checking the time. The fact he didn't use the phone in the room but went into the hallway to call the police, where I wouldn't be able to hear him well. I should have realized . . . and even when we got to Shurrock's Drift and the only other car there was Kenton's, I just couldn't think. Until you came out of the drift, Eric, and she, Dorothy — got scared. She was expecting Kenton, she couldn't make you out in the darkness, so she called his name — and then she knew it wasn't him.'

'If you *hadn't* been there, I wouldn't be alive now' Eric said quietly. He looked towards Bateman. 'Will you be charging her with attempted murder?'

Bateman cleared his throat with a touch of asperity, as though expecting criticism. 'We can't be sure that murder was in mind. They both insist they had no intention of killing you. The idea was you'd still think it was Svensson who was behind it all. They say they expected to get away with it, just leaving you there.'

'With Anne sitting in the car, handing the money over to Mrs Farnon and Kenton?' Eric asked in disbelief. 'What did they intend doing about her?'

Bateman coloured, but he had already reached his own conclusions and would not be disturbed by hypotheses, however logical. As they said, you rushed them, broke up their planning, and I really don't think they would have killed—'

'That's *your* theory,' Eric said stiffly. He hesitated as he felt a faint prickling at the back of his eyes, a recurrent nightmare of the way he had sweated in the cold blackness, of the blood running down his wrists, of the thrusting against the baulk of timber and of the whistling sound in the tunnel, the soft, triumphant singing of 'The Blaydon Races.' It had been the sound of a man coming to do something he was going to enjoy doing . . . something he had *always* enjoyed doing.

Nor had there been anything indecisive in the way Dorothy Farnon had held that screwdriver, even though she had been persuaded to drop it when the situation was obviously hopeless. Eric glanced at Anne. She was staring at him, wide-eyed. He wanted to argue with Bateman, but Anne had been through enough. He bit back the words. Instead, he asked, 'Where does this leave Scarn? I've decided not to continue working for him, of course.'

Bateman rose to his feet, expanded his barrel chest importantly. He regarded the bandages on Eric's hands and wrists, contemplated the deep scratch on his face where the gag had been torn away by the falling timber, and his bigot's mouth twisted. 'Scarn? I don't suppose you *could* work for him in this condition anyway. As to what happens to him — the answer is: nothing. He's committed no criminal offence . . . yet. He's still a thorn in O'Connor's side, of course. Reilly will be going down on a murder charge but I have a feeling he won't give us enough evidence to haul in O'Connor as well. So we'll be leaving Scarn and O'Connor to needle each other and I'd agree that Tyneside isn't big enough for both of them — something will blow in the end. Same with the local government corruption investigations. Something will crawl out of the woodwork in due course . . . it always does. All we have to do is wait . . .'

* * *

After Bateman had gone, Anne sat on the floor in front of Eric, watching him quietly. In a little while, to exorcise the demons in his head, Eric said, 'I meant what I said about your being there at Shurrock's Drift: Dorothy Farnon was set to run me down: she was so panic-stricken she'd have killed me herself.'

'So I saved your life.' She smiled. '*Now* will you marry me?'

'I still have my doubts.'

'I don't.'

He smiled. 'All right. Maybe it is time I made an honest woman of you.'

'I can set a date?'

'We'll set a date,' he agreed.

They were silent for a while, at ease with each other, but then it all came trickling back into Eric's mind: the suspicions he had held about Carter, the Quayside stallholder; about the publican Fenchurch — and about Svensson. He thought of his refusal to listen to common sense and logic; his denial of the assurances Bateman had given him; and he remembered the injuries Fred Lock had suffered . . .

He rose abruptly and walked across the room. He poured himself a glass of Scotch from the decanter, making an exception to general habit. He sipped the whisky, aware of what was in Anne's eyes but unable to dispel the shadow that Detective-Superintendent Bateman had left with him. Leave the matter to us, Bateman had said. Eric Ward hadn't done that. He'd acted, even though his knowledge had been minimal, his vision limited.

'It's not so,' Anne said softly, understanding. 'You were *not* responsible for the death of that girl, in Byker.'

'No,' he lied, for her. 'No, I really don't think I was.'

THE END

FREE KINDLE BOOKS

Please join our mailing list for free Kindle crime thriller, detective, mystery, romance books and new releases, as well as news on the next book by Roy Lewis! www.joffebooks.com

Thank you for reading this book. If you enjoyed it please leave feedback on Amazon or Goodreads, and if there is anything we missed or you have a question about then please get in touch. The author and publishing team appreciate your feedback and time reading this book.

We're very grateful to eagle-eyed readers who take the time to contact us. Please send any errors you find to corrections@joffebooks.com

ALSO BY ROY LEWIS

ERIC WARD MYSTERIES
Book 1: *The Sedleigh Hall Murder*
Book 2: *The Farming Murder*
Book 3: *The Quayside Murder*

INSPECTOR JOHN CROW
Book 1: *A Lover Too Many*
Book 2: *Error of Judgment*
Book 3: *The Woods Murder*
Book 4: *Murder for Money*
Book 5: *Murder in the Mine*
Book 6: *A Cotswolds Murder*
Book 7: *A Fox Hunting Murder*
Book 8: *A Dartmoor Murder*